Married by Twelfth Night
Anneka R. Walker

To five talented writers and kindred spirits (my critique group): Mindy Strunk, Sally Britton, Laura Beers, Heidi Kimball, and Laura Rollins.

My books are better because they pass through your hands.

Thank you for laughing at the jokes in my stories. It's too late to change your mind about them—they're memorialized in print.

Chapter 1

November 1814

London, England

READING A WILL PRIOR to the person's death was like determining the winner of a duel before the swords had ever been drawn. Where was the logic? The traditional order of events? Indeed, Richard's Great Aunt Edith had no idea what sort of chaos she had invoked upon her family. Neither he nor his cousins sitting in Mr. Davidson's stuffy solicitor's office had been prepared for the sorry news of their aunt's health, but they had been equally unprepared to learn there were *conditions* they'd be required to fulfill if they desired a share in her vast fortune.

Richard leaned toward his cousin Colin Birchall, who sat tall and stoic beside him. "She won't ask us to sacrifice any limbs, right?"

His cousin gave him a bored look.

It was a bad joke, but the tension in the room was mounting, and he could hardly stand it. The stress he'd carried this last year was like a bad dream he couldn't wake up from. And now Aunt Edith was dying—a woman he greatly respected and loved.

Mr. Davidson lifted a stack of letters in his right hand. "I will now pass out a personal letter to each of you explaining the terms of your aunt's will." The short man stepped out behind his desk and extended a sealed note to Richard before moving down the line to the others. "We tailored each letter to your individual circumstances. Go ahead and open them."

Richard desperately needed money to save his estate, but his hand hovered over the seal on the folded cream paper. His mother and sister had not yet discovered the dire situation they were in. After all these generations, he hated that he could be the one to lose it. Aunt was known for her eccentric ways, but would she leave him the money he needed to save it?

Richard curiously observed the others rip into their letters first, not ready to learn his fate. His cousin Alden Dandridge pushed away from the window he'd been leaning against. "Scotland?" His wide eyes bored into his letter.

The small, crowded room grew silent. Much too silent.

The solicitor moved to quietly explain to Alden his situation.

Richard had once heard of Aunt's horse farm in Scotland, and he felt relieved that Alden would be responsible for it instead of him. He had enough problems at home to deal with. Richard knew he shouldn't delay his own set of terms. Uncertainty formed a pit in his stomach as he broke the seal and unfolded the letter.

My darling nephew,

You have been neglecting me, and you are fortunate that my generous manner has allowed me to overlook such a matter. Regardless of your failings, I am dying, and I ought to make one last mark on the world before I go. The fact of the matter is, you need money and I have it in spades. Since I cannot purchase even a feather in heaven, and have no children of my own, it behooves me to bestow my riches upon my three unmarried grandnephews and my eldest unmarried grandniece.

You, my dear Richard, might have asked for a loan earlier, but I see you are too proud for such a favor. No one likes to admit when one's estate is not up to snuff. However, yours is rich with history and ought to be preserved. Unfortunately, the time for loans from me is over, and I cannot offer you such. Don't take any blame on yourself for this sorry situation. Before you ever inherited it, the estate at Belside was land rich and cash poor. These things happen to even the very best of people.

My solution is simple. I will give you 20,000 pounds to pay off any debts, invest in updated farm equipment and livestock, and sustain the estate until the land reaches a sustainable level again. I only have one small request: You must marry! The deed must take place by Twelfth Night. And a caution to you—unless you have any favors from the archbishop, it would be wise to remember that it takes three weeks to post the banns for a proper wedding. See that it is done!

"Twelfth Night?" he hissed. "That's impossible!" Richard lowered the letter into his lap, unable to continue with the flood of thoughts and the rising tide of emotions within him. Belside Manor could be saved! He wanted to leap from his seat and embrace his aunt. But marry? And in such short a time? This nonsensical idea hammered him firmly down in his seat and made him want to hug himself instead.

"I am expected to attend a house party for Christmas—with strangers." His cousin Rose Portman scoffed over her own letter, her bright-blue eyes wide with consternation.

"That doesn't sound like you," Alden said, blowing a lock of dark hair off his forehead.

No, it didn't. Rose despised social gatherings and all the insipid, meaningless conversation.

Colin shook his head. "It's a lot of money, and I know we all need it, but marry? In so short a time?"

While his cousins were struggling over their requests, he was too consumed with his own problems to give them any reassurance. Richard hadn't spent more than a second or two contemplating marriage. He knew he would get around to it eventually, but he had wanted to live a little more before tying himself down. Could he do this? For the sake of his family and his estate?

His jaw set, and determination steeled over him.

He had to try.

Keep reading, Richard. He could almost hear his aunt warning him to not be self-assured quite yet. Reluctantly, he raised the letter back up and read.

I know this feels sudden. But if I had one dying wish, it would be to see you all wed and starting families of your own. And since it is my money and my death wish, and I likely know you better than you know yourself, I have stipulations about who this wife should be!

Let it be known, I don't want any ninnies watering down the bloodline. I expect you to marry someone with intelligence. She must have a great love for reading and for discussing the great poets and philosophers. She must have a demure personality—a woman who regularly reflects upon the complexities of life since you will not take the time to do so. She will be the soft and gentle companion to balance your strength of character. Let her be pretty but not overly so. I myself am no diamond of the first water, and I much prefer the average sort. I would not want her tempted toward vanity.

It is of utmost importance that she be musical. This is a tradition carried through generations of Grahams. Your father was a great singer, like yourself, and your mother and sister exceptional pianists. I, myself, play the harpsichord very well and should like to cast my gaze down from heaven in the near future to view your posterity rivaling the choirs of angels. Do not disappoint me in this!

It should go without mention that a suitable dowry is included. Money is a necessity we cannot put our nose up at. Beyond this, I should like her family seat to be in Derbyshire, no more than twenty miles from Wetherfield. Family ties are essential to happiness, and travel is a difficulty you can avoid with minimal effort on your behalf. I happen to know of several marriageable women of esteem who reside near you, and I will not budge on this particular instruction. While I desire a love match for everyone in my family, I believe you are capable of winning anyone's heart and loving them in return.

I beg you to take my generous offer and marry forthwith. Your estate and future depend upon it. Because I know how deeply your affection lies toward your mother and sister, I trust these funds will be used for their welfare as well. Instead of setting aside monies for their benefit, I leave their caretaking completely in your capable hands.

Do not forget your deadline! God be with us both in these coming weeks.

If he had felt sick upon learning of the financial state of Belside after his father's death, this letter made him feel far worse. The solution to all his problems dangled before him, but it was just beyond his reach. He could not think of a single woman of his acquaintance who fit this . . . this absurd fantasy that Aunt had created for him. But no other solution in the last fifteen months had presented itself to him, despite the long hours of meeting with his own solicitor and the banks, as well as seeking counsel from friends. He had never taken life very seriously before, and the gap in his education and in running and sustaining an estate was vast.

But no ready answer had come. He'd already shut up a whole wing of the house so they would not have to warm it for the winter, but he knew it would not be enough. Aunt's will could be his saving grace.

He rubbed a hand over his jaw. How was a man to meet a woman local to his home and so particularly skilled? Mr. Green, a family friend from Wetherfield, always held a ball on the first of December, heralding in the winter season. It was a week away and the soonest event he could think of. He didn't always attend, but this year, he would not miss it. It would be the perfect opportunity to find a wife.

And if there was no opportunity, he would have to make one.

Aunt Edith had issued one challenge he could not turn down.

Chapter 2

December 1814

Wetherfield, Derbyshire

IT WAS IMPOSSIBLE TO hide from a man in a ballroom. Grace had tried and failed. Unsuccessfully, she had circled the interior perimeter, weaving around chattering acquaintances and friends, barely one step ahead of Mr. Dobson. Not even the bust Mr. Green had commissioned of himself, and its accompanying pedestal, had the dimensions to conceal a person.

Looking over her shoulder, her satin-gloved hands tightened into fists. He was nearly upon her. The only foreseeable solution was to flee the room entirely. Clenching the skirt of her gown, she maneuvered around a table holding a dazzling winter bouquet and reached the door to the corridor. Ready to bolt through it, Grace made the mistake of turning her head and catching her mother's eye. Mama, wearing her favorite pearls, gave a decisive shake of her head followed by a steely glare. It wasn't fair. Mama wanted Grace to be caught. She didn't care by whom, so long as the captor was decently respectable and wedding vows followed. Grace was far more particular.

But heed her mother, she must.

The only way Grace was getting a Season in London with her aunt was through good behavior.

Taking a reluctant step back into the fray of twirling skirts and roaming couples, Grace found herself face-to-face with *him*. Mr. Dobson. Her relentless pursuer. His dark hair was slicked back with pomade and his grin clownish. His gaze raked her up and down as if he had cornered a coveted prize.

"Miss Steele," he wheezed, winded from the chase.

Her whole body sighed. "Yes, Mr. Dobson?"

"We were talking about the future . . . our future, when you disappeared from my side."

She couldn't have given him a more blatant hint about how she felt about any future that included the both of them. "The ballroom is hardly the place for such a discussion, sir."

"Sir?" Mr. Dobson smoothed back the hair just above his ear, as if any hair dared escape the thick paste freezing it into place. "Call me Rufus."

She would die first. "That would hardly be appropriate, Mr. Dobson. As to our future, you must not have heard me when I said I was not interested in a relationship with you."

"Interest is hardly a prerequisite. Your father and mine are old family friends. It's expected of us."

An ugly fear settled on her shoulders. Who was expecting it? This was the first she had ever heard about it. Was that why her mother had quelled her escape with one of her icy parental stares?

Mr. Dobson tiptoed closer. The action was ridiculous. He was ridiculous. If he said the word marriage, she wouldn't recover, but she knew the word hovered on his slimy mouth. But he wouldn't stop there. No, he would ask her father for her hand, and Papa would remember his good friend and have no reason to turn him down.

"I cannot continue this discussion, Mr. Dobson." She stepped back, desperately searching the crowded room for someone to rescue her. "Excuse me."

That's when she saw it, her unwitting savior: Richard Graham. He looked the part of a hero without any effort of his own. Her eyes quickly took his measure with the smallest amount of begrudging admiration. One hand rested on his narrow hips as he gave a rich laugh, evoking the same gleeful emotion to his circle of friends. His long legs competed with his broad shoulders like a game where both finished triumphant. His thick brown hair, always a little tousled, lent his superior appearance a bit of ruggedness.

Everyone fawned over him, but she refused to do so. It grieved her that it had to be him. But desperate times called for drinking the bitter dregs of humility. Richard would aid her. He was good-tempered, and she had practically grown up in his house alongside his younger sister, Bridget. But she took a great risk in giving him an allowance to tease her. She preferred to have the upper hand, and it pained her to give him any fodder to use against her.

"Excuse me, Mr. Dobson. I see my partner for the next set." Grace didn't mince her steps in retreat but marched boldly to Richard's side. A foot from her target, she wavered for a single breath. This was Richard. The same man who had neglected his sister after the loss of his father. The thought still rankled her and made her want to kick him instead of greet him like a lady.

Mr. Dobson's penetrating gaze on her back chased away any hesitancy. The kicking could be postponed. There was hardly enough room for a person between Richard and his companions, but her petite size worked in her favor. Placing herself firmly beside him, she stopped herself just shy of slipping her hand into the crook of his arm. She had to make a point, but she wasn't that desperate.

Was it too much to ask that he simply ignore her? She had given him plenty of reason to do so with her behavior toward him over the years. All he had to do was let her hide under his protection. A simple, extremely minor, favor.

Not a second later, Richard looked down at her with his fair blue eyes, meeting her gaze square on. So much for ignoring her. At least he had the sense not to look appalled. He did quirk a subtle, curious brow that anyone else would have missed.

"Miss Steele? Such a rare fortune to catch you by my side." He flashed her his famous, charismatic smile that left women swooning a county over.

That same smile normally made her grimace. No one man should hold the charm of ten. It was selfish and wasted on a single person. She slid a smile across her own mouth, one undoubtedly far less striking. "Mr. Graham, I apologize for keeping you waiting."

"I was waiting for you?"

Her smile lowered a notch, and she barely kept from glaring at him. "Indeed. You desired to speak to me?"

"Did I?"

She sensed several sets of eyes on her, including Mr. Dobson's. He had crept closer and now hovered a few feet away. He hadn't given up. Why wouldn't he give up?

"You did," she said, forcing her smile to widen again, only managing to make it twitch. Oh, botheration. Couldn't the man play along for a single minute? Close friends could share a look and communicate a lifetime, but she and Richard had never been close in that sort of way. In fact, the physical distance between them now was likely the closest to date. He had a suffocating air about him, and she preferred to keep a respectable distance at all times.

When he didn't respond directly, she added, "Don't you recall? You said it was of *utmost* importance." She thought quickly. She didn't care to paint herself into a picture where people saw the two of them as a couple, but she did need something convincing. If she wasn't so flustered by Mr. Dobson, she would have thought of something straightaway. She blurted the first thing she could think of. "Let me remind you. It was something about a request from your mother."

Richard's mother's health hadn't been the same since his father's death, and she hardly left her bed. By some miracle, and a great deal of persuading, Mrs. Graham had agreed to visit Bath with a friend in hopes the change of setting and doctors would help. They all hoped partaking of the waters would aid her recovery. Few knew how poorly her spirits had been outside the Grahams, but Grace knew. And Richard knew she knew. The word "mother" was like a secret code, and something flashed across his eyes in response to it.

"Forgive me, I had momentarily forgotten." He stepped back from his friends. "Excuse us, please."

She assumed Richard would pull her toward an open section along the back of the room, but he led her toward the French doors bearing fragrant wreaths of wine-colored roses with sprigs of snowdrops, directing her outside the one already open side. A man had never pulled her onto a balcony before, but she let the satisfaction of having Mr. Dobson witness the moment appease any concern niggling her.

Cool night air brushed the width of skin between her gloves and her short-puffed bishop's sleeves and curled around her neck, refreshing her senses from the heat of the ballroom. Richard stopped away from the few couples lined along the balustrade and leaned against the white marble stone gleaming in the moonlight.

"What are you scheming now, Gracie May?"

That look, along with her childhood nickname, should have made her feel guilty, but she was only grateful for the rescue. She hadn't had time to make a full-fledged plan, but she had to explain herself. She only needed a minute to think. "Scheming is a strong word, *Richie* Graham."

Stating his name, like he had done hers, made her feel like they were on equal footing. She was probably the only one in the world who dared call him such, but he'd never grown out of calling her by her childhood nickname and used it whenever they were out of earshot of others. Turning it around on him seemed justifiably fair.

He chuckled like he saw right through her clever attempt to rattle him. "Whatever it is, you must be desperate if you're using my mother's name in one of your nefarious plans."

"I would never use your mother ill. Her name was employed out of *desperation*."

"Gracie, desperate? By all means, tell me everything." When his amused gaze met hers, she shivered. He misinterpreted her physical reaction and added, "But do keep it brief. We wouldn't want you to catch cold and keep you from your grand plans."

"I'm not cold," she said, truthfully, although it was worth noting that he seemed sincerely concerned about her health. His generosity was the one reason she could never hate him. "I shivered because the necessity of this conversation displeases me. You were the best I could do at the moment."

His eyes sparked in what could only be further amusement. "How very kind of you to convince me to leave my friends so you could criticize me in private."

"Keep your voice down, if you please. I meant it as a way of explanation. I need a favor."

That word elicited a reaction. Richard folded his arms, emphasizing the broadness of his chest and how perfectly opposite he was to Mr. Dobson's squirrelly body. "I'm listening."

Her mind jumped to an easy solution. "I need you to ask me to dance."

Richard's mouth quirked as he worked to suppress a laugh. "This is your desperate cause?"

She nodded, not caring to explain that she hadn't had time to concoct something better and was improvising. Why make herself look worse than she already did?

"I wonder how I am so fortunate to be your partner of choice. Aren't you the one who told Miss Harrington last fall that I danced like an elephant?"

She chewed her bottom lip. "It was a calculated response made out of my affection for your sister. Miss Harrington had her eyes set on you, and Bridget did not deserve to be strapped with such a foolish sister-in-law for the rest of her life."

He nodded, but not like he believed her. "Foolish, you say? That reminds me of how I felt when you pinned a note to the back of my jacket with the word ignorant on it."

She cast her eyes to the inky sky in exasperation. "That was two years ago over a very poor remark you made about the general capabilities of my gender. How was I supposed to know you were on your way to meet with friends?" Must he bring up her every transgression? She would never admit it, but the cool breeze had started to chill her. This was taking much too long to convince him.

His eye narrowed and his mouth curled. "Oh, I think you knew perfectly well what you were doing then and now. You're always scheming something. I'm not certain this request for a dance is not a trap."

Perhaps she had known that he was to see his friends that day she'd pinned a note to him, but she was generally good-natured and trustworthy. "Everything I do is not so calculated. You cannot even think of a current example." His expectant, pointed look forced her to clear her throat and regather her argument. "No harm will come to your person this time, *I promise.*"

He shifted against the marble. "Ah, but your honesty leaves little to be desired."

Her hand slid to her hip. "What is that supposed to mean?"

"It means I have plenty of current examples of your ill will toward me. Where to begin?"

Grace swallowed, glancing at the other couples braving the cold and milling about. "Do you have the time? I think we ought to return inside."

His words barreled forward, completely dismissive of her own. "Just a few weeks ago, you told Miss Thorne that my reading voice sounded like the snores of a hibernating bear."

Drat! So he heard about that, had he? "She knew I was close to your sister and asked for a list of your qualities. I said a few redeeming things as well . . . I think." She straightened. "Would you have me lie?"

He shrugged. "You expect me to be flattered by all this honesty?"

She should have apologized, or even begged, but she had never been very good at either. "Flattered, no, but understanding, yes. It's you or Mr. Dobson, and can't I prefer the lesser evil of the two?"

"Mr. Dobson?" His eyes lit up like a fire consuming the yule log. "What a fine catch you have ensnared."

She winced. The truth was out. He knew her weakness. "I have no desire to couple my name with his, but he is quite determined. He cannot corner me if we are dancing, and the night is almost over. You will not have to stay by my side after the set is finished." She paused, waiting for him to respond. "So . . . will you do it?"

His eyes glimmered like he was doing a math problem and was pleased with the solution. "And you will owe me what?"

"Anything!" she blurted.

"Ah, I like that sound of that." The smoldering intensity of his words and expression made her worry she'd promised too much. But this was Mr. Dobson they were speaking about. Avoiding him was worth a great deal of sacrifice.

Dazzling white snowflakes broke their taut gaze. "The first snow," she whispered. No one would deem her a romantic, but her older sister Ruth once told her that witnessing the first snow with a man was a sign of true love. But since Grace was viewing it with Richard, she took it as a sign of foreboding.

Richard pushed away from the balustrade. "Our cue to return inside. Lead the way, Gracie May."

There it was. His pet name for her reminded her that she was but a child to him, which was made worse with a rhyme. Still, a real smile slipped free at the corners of her mouth. She would never admit it, but that name that she'd tried desperately to despise was actually her favorite part about Richard Graham. After all the harmless teasing, there was loyalty and unspoken respect between them that meant they would never push too far. She would have to repay the favor at some point, but he wouldn't ask anything impossible of her. No, he valued her relationship with his sister too much. At least she had that small comfort.

Chapter 3

RICHARD HADN'T TIME FOR games, but the clock ticked steadily in his mind since he'd arrived at the ball and suddenly slowed when he'd pulled Grace outside. The rush of chilly winter air had opened his eyes. He didn't have to solve his problems alone. Grace could help him. Vexing but, oh, so intelligent Grace. When she wasn't out to skewer him with her words, she could be rather brilliant.

No one else could have convinced his mother to leave her bed and try Bath for her health. If she didn't despise him so, he might have thought of her sooner.

When they reentered the glowing ballroom, warmth radiated from the grand fireplace on the far end combined with the sheer number of Wetherfield's finest. Richard kept Grace's arm in his and moved along the wall swathed with glimmering candlelight and dancing shadows from the sparkling chandeliers.

He glanced at his silent companion, who was far too busy searching for Mr. Dobson to heed him. He slowed before reaching his friends. Could he stomach more trivial conversation and gossip? No, he didn't believe he could. He stopped abruptly, a good distance from them, content to wait alone with Grace in preparation for the next set. Oblivious to his own mental dilemmas, she dropped his arm and worried her hands together.

He attempted to put her out of her misery. "He's on your right behind the woman with the green turban."

Grace's head whipped in the direction he indicated, and she stilled. "He hasn't seen us yet."

"He's searching for you. He must have seen us come back inside." Mr. Dobson wasn't tall, but he craned his neck every which way.

"This dance cannot end and ours begin soon enough," she muttered, her lips pulling into a tight line. His eyes naturally traced her face to her pert little nose. She had always reminded him of a little pixie—naturally pretty and far too clever for her own good. Her hair was neatly pulled back in a soft but practical style. She never had loose tendrils by her face; no, she was too sensible to let her hair obscure her smart greenish-blue eyes. They were the stage of her face where everything was dreamed up and executed. One could watch it happen like an expertly crafted play, usually with plenty of wit, and if it included him, a hint of artifice.

Grace was Bridget's dearest friend, and thankfully, she treated his sister far better than she treated him. For that reason, he had tried dutifully to ignore her through the years. Unless, of course, one of her schemes made doing so impossible. This time though, the tables were turned, and she had played right into his hands.

"Gracie . . ." he began, not certain of the best way to approach the subject. "Let's start a game while we wait. You seem in need of distraction."

"Game?" Her brows lifted, and he suddenly had her full attention. That had been much too easy. But Grace had always had a knack for games, and it was only in the playing of such games that they were able to make a temporary truce and get along.

He nodded. "A riddle. I know how fond you are of those." Before university, they had exchanged several riddles, but he had worked hard to stump her—going as far as to create a list of rhyming words ten pages long. His motive was vastly opposite this time. He needed her to solve the riddle and solve it quickly.

"Go ahead," she prompted. "Let's hear it."

Richard nodded toward the dancers. "I will list a few qualities and you tell me who in this room matches my description."

Her eyes sharpened—like a turbulent sea beginning to settle. He could never tell if her eyes were more green or blue since both shades were swirled together, but right now they were decidedly blue.

Excellent. Grace would tell him exactly which woman in this room would be his future bride.

He added a few rhyming words to Aunt's list of requirements:

Unattached and well-read, with music I share;
Mild in my looks, with a keen, thoughtful air.
Who am I?

Grace grinned. "Simple. Mrs. Kemp."

His own mouth dipped into a frown. "Mrs. Kemp? The widow, Mrs. Kemp?"

She nodded. "No one fits the description better."

He scratched the fine scruff on his jaw. Was he prepared to wed a buxom woman ten years his senior with a brood of seven children? Could he do it to save Belside Manor? He shook his head. "She isn't exactly who I had in mind."

"There aren't many others who fit your qualifications with perfect accuracy. Miss Ryder wouldn't know the difference between Aristotle and Byron, but she sings like a lark. Miss Delworth is quite her opposite. Let me think. I do love a good riddle."

At least someone here did. He hadn't thought of a single candidate who would fit Aunt's incredibly specific list. "Keep thinking, Gracie.

If anyone can discover the answer, it is you." And if she couldn't, he and his home were doomed.

Mr. Dobson spotted them at that moment. Richard shifted closer to Gracie, hoping to give an air of possessiveness to deter his flight of pursuit. As soon as he did it, he wondered at his motivation. He had agreed to a dance and no more. They weren't exactly friends, he and Grace Steele, but he wouldn't call them enemies either. Somewhere in between would be the clear diagnosis of whatever they suffered from when in each other's company. But even as he thought through his reasoning, he could not deny his desire to protect her. Mr. Dobson wasn't a despicable man, but he had very little sense. And as such, there was not a man more disqualified to court Gracie.

Just as the violins played the final notes of a quadrille, a moment before Mr. Dobson reached them, Grace snapped her fingers. "I have it! I don't know how I didn't see it before."

Richard didn't wait to hear her answer. A simple country dance was announced, and the music began again. He wasted no time in tucking Grace's arm in his and whisking her toward the couples lining up for the next set. Glancing back, he saw Mr. Dobson's glare of annoyance. He sent a smug smile of satisfaction over his shoulder at him, drawing Grace closer.

A moment later, they reached the end of the line, and he released her and stepped across from her.

"Well?" she spoke. "Don't you want to hear my answer to your riddle?"

He hesitated for the briefest moment, preparing himself for the worst. "Yes, I do."

"My sister."

His brow furrowed. "Your sister?" he repeated.

She nodded. "Ruth would rather be in the library than any other room in the house, and she is very dedicated to the pianoforte."

He bowed to her when the music cued him to, and she dipped into a curtsy. He didn't have a chance to continue the discussion about Grace's older sister Ruth once the dance began, but he hadn't needed to. He knew her from years of sharing neighboring estates. Perhaps claiming to know her was a bit of a stretch. She was shy, painfully so. Aunt had required this mystery woman to possess a softer, gentler nature, which seemed to be Ruth exactly.

As far as the rest of the list, Ruth matched there as well. She was rather plain in comparison to Grace, but not in a way that repelled him. And there was no reason to worry about the vicinity of her residence. Their families were more likely to see too much of them than too little.

The Steeles had always been family friends, and a marriage between them, while never pursued in conversation or thought, would not be wholly shocking. The Steeles would probably be delighted with the arrangement and would benefit from the slightly raised social connection. Which led him to wonder about Ruth's dowry. It shouldn't be too hard to learn with all his trips to Callis Hall. Mr. Steele had been tutoring him on a few of the many business aspects behind running an estate.

Grace gave a breathless grin as she whirled around, and he felt his own lips pull at the corner. It amused him to see her enjoying their dance. Would Ruth enjoy it too? She was musical, after all. He tried to visualize her dancing but realized he had never asked Ruth to dance before and did not recall seeing her on the dance floor either.

Surely, she would look as much a picture as her sister.

Yes, Miss Ruth Steele would do. He had done it. Or rather, *Grace* had done it. He had found the woman he would marry.

Chapter 4

GRACE'S MAID, KATIE, SHOVED another pin into Grace's boring brown coiffure, trying to force the stubbornly straight hair to stay where she wanted it to. She gave Katie a look of apology just as Mama entered her bedchamber with the same exuberance as her fourteen-year-old brother, Tobias. Through the mirror she could see Mama smiled a little too bright, and her eyes were much too awake after the late night.

Something wasn't quite right. "What is it, Mama?"

"Nothing. Nothing at all. Can't a mother come and tell her daughter good morning?"

She gave a partial shrug so not to mess with the careful sculpting of her hair. "If she never enters my room at such an hour and does so suddenly, it cannot be without suspicion." Mama's affronted expression made her laugh. "I'm teasing. Mostly. Tell me what makes you so cheerful."

Mama came to her side so they did not have to talk through the mirror. "I want to know everything that happened last night. I couldn't ask last night with your father in the carriage."

Papa thought Mama too excitable about topics of courtship, while she was convinced that if not for her efforts and persuading, her two daughters would volunteer for a life of spinsterhood. If Mama, in her anxiety to see them married off, insisted Grace accept Mr. Dobson's attention, she would consider running away to her aunt's in London. Her eyes flicked to the letter on her desk with Aunt's invitation to join her after the holidays—an invitation she had to cleverly extricate—and remembered how Mama had soundly rejected the idea. She wanted Grace to stay with Ruth, and even though Grace was younger, Mama desired her to be a companion to her sister until one of them married. Which could be a very, very long time.

Only the best behavior would persuade Mama to change her mind.

With resignation, Grace asked the question, "What about last night?" She tucked an unruly wisp of hair into her bun and braced herself for Mama's answer.

Mama tsked. "Don't play coy with me. I saw it all."

"Then what could I possibly say to satisfy you?"

Mama folded her arms tightly across her small chest. They were both of similar build, and she wondered if she would someday stare crossly at her own daughter that way, like the whole of her person brimmed with annoyance. "I'm speaking about Mr. Graham."

"Richard?" she frowned. "What do you want to know about *him*?"

"For the last time. He is not a boy. He must be referred to as *Mr. Graham.*"

She hadn't intended to slip his given name, especially while she was doing her best to earn Mama's favor. "Yes, Mama," she said obediently. What would Mama have said if Grace had accidentally called him Richie?

"Mr. Graham," Mama began, "paid you marked attention last night. I was not the only one to notice. Mrs. Meecham saw it too."

She squinted trying to remember how she had given this impression. She had tried to send a message with Richard's presence to Mr. Dobson and him alone. But she had been extremely careful with her words to his friends. What could her mother be worried about? What had Mrs. Meecham seen too?

She replayed the night in her mind and her eyes slowly widened. The balcony. The tight way she'd gripped his arm. The way he'd pulled her close as they walked toward the dancers. She gripped her dressing table. Good heavens. Anyone could have misconstrued the whole thing.

"It was nothing," she said quickly.

Too quickly.

Mama's brow lifted. "There is no understanding between you two?"

"Understanding? He danced with me for one set. How did your mind jump to an understanding? Really, Mama. You know how I abhor the man. You are too hasty." She didn't hate him exactly, but it was harder to put to words the constant state of annoyance his presence brought to her. The only real understanding she had with Richard was the one created in their youth. It was her job to humble him and his to tease her mercilessly. Nothing more, nothing less.

Mama shrugged one shoulder. "Am I being hasty? Or are you hiding something? You are at Belside often enough to change your opinion of the man."

"There is nothing to hide. You are attempting to create a love match out of one insignificant dance. Richard—"

"Mr. Graham." This time there was no censure in her voice, only curiosity.

"Mr. Graham," she corrected, "barely tolerates me. He, no doubt, favored me with his company out of duty to his sister."

Mama shook her head. "A man doesn't do such favors for sisters that are not even in attendance."

Need Mama remind her of the sore topic? Her dearest friend Bridget was not out in Society yet but at no fault of her own. It had been delayed after her father's death and now because of her mother's health. Bridget was permitted to attend dinner parties on occasion, but her mother had insisted against any balls until she could be her chaperone and guide.

Grace and Bridget were only two years apart in age, but Grace had had three years of Society already. Moments like last night made it feel like three years too many. Before she could defend herself again to Mama, a second maid knocked.

"Mr. Dobson is here to pay a call on Miss Grace," the maid said.

She pressed her eyes shut. Why? Why was this happening to her?

"Splendid," Mama said, slapping her hands against her thighs.

That one word made Grace pry her eyes back open. "Splendid?"

"Yes. If there is no understanding with Mr. Graham, perhaps you can secure one with Mr. Dobson."

Grace balked, twisting in her chair. "What about Ruth? Why are you not in her bedchamber this morning? Let's send *her* down to see Mr. Dobson." She didn't want Ruth to suffer either, but she was older. Wasn't it her responsibility?

"You know Ruth is shy."

Another reason Grace had to stay by her very capable sister's side. "She does not like company, but she is not so very shy."

Mama shook her head, moving to the door. "I depend on you to marry well to bring attention to your sister."

Her? Marry well? What a laughable joke. She hadn't been ready to marry in years past and had managed to chase away any decent suitors. She had realized the error of her ways too late, and she knew she would have to seek a husband outside of Wetherfield if such a union should ever come into existence. She sighed. "And an alliance with Mr. Dobson is your definition of marrying well?"

"Grace Steele, I won't have you speak of that nice man like that. He is from a trusted family. He only needs a good wife to make him shine."

Grace thought of his slicked back hair and grumbled, "He shines well enough on his own."

"That's the spirit." Mama set her hand on the door frame. "Hurry and put on your slippers and meet us in the drawing room. I will distract him until you're ready. Katie, when you are finished with the hair, find Ruth and instruct her to join us."

What Grace wouldn't give in the moment to trade places with her brother Tobias. He was so lucky to be born a man with more say in his future. Like any smart adolescent, he was likely hiding in some corner of the house so Mama could give all her nagging attention to his older sisters.

Grace hurried to finish her toilette but only so she could have the visit over with all the sooner. She intended to visit Bridget and relay all the miserable details. No one would sympathize more.

Sunlight poured through the windows a few minutes later, greeting Grace as she entered the drawing room. With all the added sunshine, the room had not quite warmed despite the crackling fire behind the grate. It was a dire shame the cold temperatures outside had not kept Mr. Dobson at home.

Mr. Dobson stood in front of one of the two rose-pink sofas in the room and dipped into a rushed bow.

Grace curtsied, with considerably less enthusiasm. She avoided Mr. Dobson's gaze and moved to Mama's side on the opposite sofa. This was all her fault. If she had learned the skills of flirtation, or rather, been less herself and more someone more refined, she might have had better options than the man in front of her.

"Did you enjoy the ball last night, Miss Steele?" Mr. Dobson sat, his posture rigid like a statue.

"It was tolerable."

Mama elbowed her.

She forced a pleasant tone and some semblance of a smile. "And you, Mr. Dobson?"

"Our dance was my favorite of the night." The sudden gleam of his eyes matched the sheen of his slicked-back hair.

She kept her smile frozen in place for Mama's sake, but inwardly, she squirmed and shivered. This conversation was getting out of hand already, and the tea things hadn't even arrived.

Ruth made a timely appearance with a book in front of her face.

"Ruth? Dear?" Mama said. "We have company."

Ruth lowered her book so her eyes could be seen. She looked like a caught mouse.

Mama frowned at her evident surprise. "Did Katie not tell you we were waiting for you?"

Katie came up behind Ruth, panting. "There you are, miss."

"Never mind, Katie. She is here now. That will be all."

Katie departed and Mama motioned for Ruth to take the open seat next to Mr. Dobson. Ruth did so but kept her book up in front of her face like a shield between them. Grace instantly felt sorry for her—for both Ruth and Mr. Dobson. And a little jealous she didn't have a book too.

Mama made a hand motion signaling for Ruth to lower the book. She did, but with a great deal of reluctance. "Ruth, dear, tell Mr. Dobson about what you've been reading. I am sure he would be happy to hear it."

"I would?" Mr. Dobson cleared his throat. "I would."

Well, done, Mr. Dobson. Grace bit back her laugh.

Mr. Reed, who had never seemed a more dutiful butler than in that moment, stepped in the doorway. His timely appearance hid her slipping smile.

"What is it, Mr. Reed?" Mama asked.

"Mr. Graham is here, Mrs. Steele."

Mama's eyes lit like a candle. "Truly? How wonderful." She reached over and squeezed Grace's hands. If Mr. Dobson had not been here, she expected Mama might have squealed with sheer delight.

Grace tried not to roll her eyes. He was likely coming to see Papa. That was the only reason he ever came to Callis Hall.

Everyone stood and heralded Mr. Graham's arrival.

"Good morning," Mr. Graham said cheerfully. "I hope I am not interrupting."

"Not at all, Mr. Graham," Mama said, trumping him in enthusiasm. "Move over, Grace, and make room."

Grace didn't move. "You are not here for my father?" she asked, giving Richard his opening to escape.

He shook his head, his eyes a tad mischievous. "Not at all. I had hoped to visit with the Misses Steeles, and I am pleased to see you are receiving guests."

Something wasn't right. Graham never visited with her or her sister. He only ever came to talk about estate business with Papa or whatever else it was men discussed. Despite the suspicions that were no doubt written on her face, Grace scooped up the excess of her flowy skirt and scooted down a cushion toward Mama.

Mr. Graham strode toward the open seat. He flipped up the back of his jacket as he sat, his great legs crossing toward her, and his arm going up to rest on the back of the sofa. Grace had the sudden urge to remind him that this was not his home, and he shouldn't act like it was.

Even if she acted like *his* home was hers on occasion.

It wasn't the same though. She had always been that way at Belside, but he was generally not around enough to care.

No one spoke for a moment. Mr. Dobson grew annoyed, Ruth bored, and Mama gleeful. Grace leaned over and whispered to Richard, "Why are you here?"

He leaned in too. "For pleasure."

She cast her gaze to the ceiling, not believing him for a moment.

"Miss Steele," Richard addressed Ruth. "With the sun shining and the last of our good days quickly waning for the year, I wonder if you would accompany me on a walk about the garden."

Ruth said nothing. Her eyes, on the other hand, said plenty. They went wide as a terrified rabbit, ready to flee for its life.

What was Richard playing at? Why did he want to walk with Ruth? It made absolutely no sense. He had never shown her the slightest interest in all these years.

"Ruth, dear," Mama prodded. "Mr. Graham asked you a question." Her brows rose multiple times and her head motioned to Mr. Graham.

Grace resisted covering her eyes with her hand, but just barely.

"I . . . I . . ." Ruth stammered, her cheeks blazing red.

"Yes!" Mama declared. "Yes, she will walk with you. Dear, send a maid to fetch your warmest cloak."

Ruth practically jumped to her feet. Her book dropped and skidded across the rug. She scrambled to retrieve it and tripped on her dress as she straightened. Her face resembled both the green and pink hues in their Axminster rug. Ruth whimpered and rushed from the room.

"I should like to walk too," Mr. Dobson said, his face full of resolve, and his small chest puffing out. "Miss Steele? Would you join me?"

"No, thank y—"

An elbow flew into her rib from Mama. Grace was tempted to pass it on to Richard for his splendid idea. She had managed well enough the night before, but she didn't generally like wandering the garden in freezing temperatures.

"Yes, Mr. Dobson." Her words came out in a long sigh. "I will return in a moment."

Grace stood with more elegance than Ruth, but the glare she speared Richard with to communicate that this was all his fault likely ruined any decorum her exit held. Instead of sending a maid to fetch their cloaks, she and Ruth both collected their own. There was no hurry for either of them to return. Grace walked as slowly as possible, stalling the inevitable while simultaneously planning how to escape Mr. Dobson. That phrase was beginning to be the theme of her life: escape Mr. Dobson. Should she extend their walk to a ridiculous length until he was both frozen and insanely bored? If only she wouldn't be plagued with the same fate.

Should she pretend to be ill? She was starting to feel the beginnings of a headache. But that wouldn't send Mr. Dobson away for good. She needed an absolute end to his attentions. This couldn't continue!

The four of them soon gathered at the front door, ready to begin their expedition. Ruth stepped behind Grace as the door swung open, as if the outside world would devour her. Grace knew otherwise. Ruth loved walking their grounds, just not with company. She felt strangely protective of her older sister and stepped more fully in front of her while she could. Ruth was a genuine person, kindhearted and sympathetic. But she had no confidence in herself and feared Society's disapproval. They were opposite in that way. Grace didn't want to displease Society, but she did not fear them. They were too flawed for her to esteem their judgments were any better than her own.

Richard led the group through the door and down the wide steps to a gravel path that ran in front of the house and circled around it. The sun was beaming, and despite the bite of cold on her cheeks, it was more tolerable than Grace expected. Mr. Dobson moved to her side. The width of the path did not allow for three people to stand side by side, forcing Ruth to step forward to join Richard.

Grace wanted to reach out and squeeze her hand, but Ruth would not have welcomed it. Her sister did have some pride, and Grace would respect it. She almost wished someone would squeeze her hand though, for her task was just as formidable as Ruth's.

Mr. Dobson let the first couple lead until there was a respectable distance between them and Grace could no longer hear the conversation ahead of them—which had been one-sided anyway, with Richard doing all the conversing. Mr. Dobson did a fair share of talking of his own but not prying speech from her like Richard was doing. Mr. Dobson spoke only of himself and his accomplishments, which included his vast collection of buttons, the detailed map he had drawn of his own garden, and the poetry he had written about his mother.

She was actually jealous of Ruth. Richard was a man of sense, no matter if he had neglected his sister in her time of need. But what could they be speaking about?

She had the next hour to wonder.

Which was not an easy feat. No number of ornamental evergreens glistening with the morning frost, or the seamless gray sky, or the excited chirping of the goldfinch in the bare treetops that lined the back garden could fully distract her from Mr. Dobson's personal oratory. He had little inflection in his voice, which she could not blame him for, as he was likely born that way. But she could blame him for his wandering hands. He kept trying to reach for her own, which she swatted away time and again.

"Mr. Dobson, it is not appropriate for you to hold my hand when we are not even engaged." She had said this twice already, in the firmest of voices, but Mr. Dobson had selective hearing.

"This can be remedied, Miss Steele." The pleasure in his voice was only noticeable because he said it louder, with more surety. "Marrying you is my family's greatest wish. I consider myself a dutiful son, and I always do as Mother tells me."

That sentence hit like a nail in the matrimonial coffin she would soon be buried in, and her anxiety mounted. Mr. Dobson would never listen to a word she said. Unless, of course, his mother approved it. If Grace did not have a plan to thwart the man by dinner, she would fast her meals until she did. This had to end! Each interaction terrified her more than the last. She would not be surprised if he made an appointment to speak with her father within the week. What had she done wrong in her life to deserve this?

"Not to mention, Miss Steele," Mr. Dobson said, "The tip of your nose reminds me of a little button. You must know my partiality toward a likeness as that. It is a sign from heaven."

Or devilish bad luck. Why couldn't Richard have come to see her instead of Ruth? She could amuse the man for an hour before sending him back to his miserable existence where he was the most important person in his own world. Perhaps that was a tad exaggerated. For the first time, she regretted haranguing him through the years. Even if it had been a most enjoyable sport. Anything was better than Mr. Dobson.

Chapter 5

RICHARD STARED AT HIS aunt's letter, reviewing the absurdly specific list of qualifications for his wife. "Utterly impossible!"

As soon as he had returned from meeting with Aunt Edith's solicitor, he had written to see if she would budge on any of the qualifications. Her response had arrived this morning and had irked him to no end.

It is my money, and I can require whatever I see fit. He dropped this new letter into his desk drawer, along with the first, and locked it away. Stashing his key under the picture frame above it, he marched to the window and leaned onto the sill.

Belside's lands sprawled before him—the pond he fished and swam in the summers, the grove of oak, ash, and beech trees where he'd built a fort with his friends, and the half-circle gravel drive where he'd left and returned a million times. This was home. *His* home. His entire world.

He massaged his right temple that was beginning to pound. Why had he been so absorbed in his own life before? Could he have helped Father with the estate instead of wasting his time with his friends or poring over useless books at Oxford? Now he was desperately courting a list instead of courting for love.

And how was it going?

His morning walk with Ruth Steele had been a disaster. She'd said no more than five words altogether. How was he supposed to marry someone who was frightened of him? There was no way he could win her over in six weeks. Correction, five weeks now.

A noise came from down the corridor toward Bridget's room. Grace must've arrived. He imagined her telling his sister about the horrors of the morning. There would be a discussion about him too—about why he had called on Ruth.

Let them speculate. No one in Wetherfield knew about Aunt's letter and no one ever would. It was better that way. He would burn it at some point to protect his future wife.

His hand lowered to the bridge of his nose, and he pinched it tight. He needed a plan to woo Ruth. A master plan. Like the time Bridget had broken the window on the house when practicing cricket with Grace a few summers back. He had warned them that Father didn't like girls playing cricket and wasn't going to be happy about it. When he'd returned from an evening with friends, he'd found the window repaired and had been threatened if he dared say anything about it.

He'd laughed at the threat. A bunch of adolescent girls didn't scare him. He told them he wouldn't tattle if they would tell him how they'd managed to fix it without Father knowing. Their plan had been one of many that had made him shake his head in wonder. They had convinced the gardener to take the window from the shed that was the same size and fit it to the house. Then they had paid the gardener for a new window for the shed that they knew Father wouldn't notice. It had been a brilliant idea.

Brilliant was what he needed right now.

Launching away from the window, he jogged across his room, threw his door open, and marched down the corridor to Bridget's room. A faint sound of voices traveled through the door. He made a fist and knocked.

Bridget pulled the door open. "Richard?" she asked warily. Her tall, willowy body leaned into the wood frame.

He donned a smile. "I thought I heard my favorite sister."

"Your only sister, need I remind you. What is it you want?

He shifted his feet. "I wondered if we might go for a walk. You, me, and Gracie."

The door widened and Grace appeared beside Bridget. Her keen eyes met his. "Don't you think you've been on enough walks today?"

Part of him was regretting this already. Why did he have to ask for help from her again? He swallowed what was left of his pride and shrugged good-naturedly. "Walking invigorates the body and mind."

Grace lifted a pointed brow. "How often does your brother take walks, Bridget?"

Bridget narrowed her eyes. "Never. He prefers to ride his horse, even if it's just across the estate."

"It's a large estate," he countered.

"Interesting," Grace said, studying him. It never seemed like a good thing to have Grace Steele appraise him. Everyone else saw what he wanted them to see, but Grace was the exception. She saw right through him and exposed all his flaws.

His mouth pulled up at one corner. "See anything you like?"

Another girl would have blushed, but she frowned.

It was the exact reaction he had intended but not the reaction he required if he were to get what he had come for. He backpedaled. He needed to stay on her good side if he were to convince her to help him. "I'm turning a new leaf and becoming an expert walker. So, will you join me?"

"I think it's too cold," Bridget said. "What do you think, Grace?"

"I agree, but I think your brother is up to something, and we ought to find out what."

He tapped the side of his leg. Grace was already sniffing out the truth. She couldn't help herself. Despite his time away at university, he'd had their youth and the time since his return to cross paths with Grace over and over again. He knew her better than most—the slight narrowing of her eyes and the barely perceptible scrunch of skin between her brows—they were her tells.

"I think you're right," Bridget said. "How about a walk to the library, Richard? We can have cook send up some sandwiches. Not quite so invigorating a distance, but will it appease you?"

He lazily folded his arms across his chest. "If this is a rematch of cribbage, then I suppose I'm up for it." He tried not to spend very much time with Grace. Managing to keep a strong presence in Society was no easy feat under the mounting pressure of his finances, and he didn't relish the little pixie seeing through his facade and calling him out. But every once in a while, he did attempt to be a good brother.

Cribbage had been his last attempt—though admittedly, it had been several months ago. He'd been so consumed with the affairs of the estate that he could hardly believe so much time had passed. And of course, Grace had been involved that day. She was everywhere Bridget was.

"Overestimating your abilities again?" Grace smirked. "By all means, lead the way."

Bridget grinned at the prospect of a competition, always a willing spectator to his losing. No one could pull a smile from her as quickly as Grace. They were more inseparable than ever lately. Strolling down the corridor toward the staircase, he stole a glance at their neighbor. Even if she drove him mad, he was eternally grateful to her. Her friendship had been the greatest comfort to his sister, and her comfort was his own. Even Mother cheered up when Grace came by. Sadly, those visits couldn't last forever, and Mother's melancholy had only progressed.

A half hour later, they were all sequestered in the library, he and Grace bent over an extended game of cribbage while Bridget wandered off to select a book from the shelf. Finally, they had bored her enough that he would have a moment's privacy with Grace.

"Grace . . . about that favor you owe me," he hedged, keeping his voice low.

Her blue-green eyes flicked from her cards up to him. "Yes?"

He hated to do this, but he was desperate. "I'm calling it in."

She put her elbow on the table and rested her head on her fist. "What do you have in mind?"

His lips twitched. Her casual posture amused him. She hadn't batted an eyelash, but she would when he told her what he had in mind. He pretended to study his cards before dragging his gaze to hers again. "I want to marry your sister."

For a moment there was no reaction, and then her brows lowered over those wide, expressive eyes. "My sister? I would never let that angelic creature near you. Is this your attempt at humor, because if so, you are worse at joking than cribbage."

He had been prepared for her surprise, but he took some offense to her word choice. "It is not a joke. Am I such a brute that I don't deserve her?"

"No one deserves her. She is too good."

Grace wasn't the only clever one. He had methods of convincing her to work with him. "If your sister marries, then the pressure will be off of you. You can leave Wetherfield."

She straightened, dropping her arm. "How do you know I want to leave Wetherfield?"

He glanced at Bridget to see if she had heard them, but her arm was propped on a pillow on the sofa and she was safely ensconced in her book. "You mentioned leaving here during our last cribbage game."

"I did?" She stared for a moment before quickly blinking away her stupor. "I mean, of course, I did. Anywhere is better than being in the same room as you."

She didn't mean it. Despite her bluster, he knew she enjoyed their interactions. Criticizing him was her finest source of entertainment. Still, he had to play along. He needed her. "You wound me, Gracie May."

"That was the point. Someone has to take you down a notch or that big head of yours might float away."

With his thumb and first finger extended, he framed his chin in his hand. "Have you been admiring my head?"

"Isn't it enough that the rest of Wetherfield does so?"

He rested his arms on the table and leaned over them. "It's enough if Ruth does so, and by the end of the holiday."

Grace's eyes sparked as if she suddenly saw a map behind his desire to marry and she had to know where it would lead. "You might as well tell me everything, Richard. You know I'll discover it on my own in the end anyway, and this will save us time."

He chewed on the inside of his cheek, debating how much to say. Bringing her into his confidence might be the only way to get her aid.

"Can you keep a secret?" He knew she could, or he never would have brought it up. No matter her opinion of him, he could trust her. After all these years, she had never told a soul about the time he'd accidentally set fire to a small section of a wheat field on their estate. She'd seen him showing off with a magnifying glass, singeing the yellow stalks ripe for the harvest. And yet, she had never tattled on him.

"I will not tell," Grace said. "But knowing your secret does not obligate me to help you."

She was smart. Too smart. "Very well, I shall tell you, but not even Bridget can know." He lowered his voice further. "Belside's estate is in trouble."

"What?" she hissed.

He quickly put his finger to her mouth, her warm lips startling him. He hadn't meant to touch her, and it was strangely hard to pull away.

"What's happened to Belside?"

Her words helped him to focus. "I inherited a nearly bankrupt estate. It needs money to survive. A lot of money."

She was silent for a long moment. He could see sorrow in her eyes, and if he dared believe it, a trace of fear. "Is that the real reason why you have closed off the west wing?"

"Yes. We cannot afford to have house guests or heat the whole house."

"I assumed your mother wanted to redecorate the rooms this winter as an excuse not to entertain."

"I wish that were the reason."

She chewed on her lower lip. "How will marrying Ruth help with that? She has a decent dowry, but if I'm correct, you need far more than what she can offer."

"A dowry would help, but you're right, I need more. My aunt is prepared to help, but only on the condition that I marry by Twelfth Night." He stopped himself before listing the stipulations. It felt uncouth to mention that he had selected her sister like one would a meal.

"And it must be Ruth?" She had that perplexed look again on her face like she was attempting to puzzle the information together but didn't quite have all the pieces yet.

"Yes, she is the one I want to marry. For Bridget's sake, and for Belside Manor, I hope you will return your favor to me and help me court your sister."

She scoffed. "It seems to me that Richard Graham has never needed any help winning a lady's favor."

"Ah, but Ruth might be the one woman in England who is afraid of me."

She frowned. "And that's why you want to marry her?"

He shook his head. "Not at all, but I would like her to *want* to marry me too."

She played with the peg on the cribbage board. "What would be expected of me?"

"Can you help me get to know her better?"

She folded her arms across her chest, her mind ticking away behind her eyes. He would beg her if he had to. His family couldn't lose Belside manor. After losing Papa, it would kill them.

"This favor isn't equal to the one I gave you," she finally said.

His heart sank.

"But I will make a deal with you."

Hope soared again. "Anything."

She smiled. "That's the same word I said to you at the ball. You might want to hear my plan first."

Indeed, he did. This was a Grace Steele plan, and it was bound to work. He leaned into the table, eager to hear it.

"You'll court me instead."

He sat back. This wasn't what he'd expected. Court Grace? His family would love it, and he . . . well, Grace was attractive, and with those keen sparking eyes, milky skin, and slender neck, she had no problem keeping his attention. But he tried to think of her as little Gracie May, the name he had come up with for her when he was probably ten, to remind himself that she was like a sister to him and not someone he should be attracted to. Besides, she would hate being married to him, and he would hate that she hated him. He wouldn't do that to her . . . or himself. Not to mention that she didn't fit any of his aunt's qualifications and would defeat his purpose. "Gracie—"

"For a few weeks, Richard. Not forever. It will allow Ruth time for her to feel safe with you, to trust you, and then your feelings will transfer to her instead."

It was a fair idea, but no, it was not worth it. He shook his head. "People will speak poorly of you. Your reputation would suffer."

"I can handle a few gossips. It's not like we would be engaged. Besides, I would be permitted to leave Wetherfield once you're married to my sister. My aunt has long promised to have me in London, and as you know, I long to go. Mama will finally realize that I have no prospects here and with a tarnished reputation, how can she say no?"

Grace could have plenty of prospects if she desired them. She had impossibly high standards, making herself seemingly unattainable. Perhaps she would be happier in London with a fresh start, but why did the idea of her leaving produce a sinking feeling in his stomach? Had he begun to feel responsible for her? She was not his sister. If she wanted to leave, she should be permitted to do so.

Selfishly, he knew his family would suffer, but so would all of Wetherfield. Grace was part of what made their slice of the countryside what it was. That's how small towns worked. They were who the people were.

"I don't know," he muttered.

She swallowed. "Would it be so hard to pretend to like me?"

The sudden vulnerability clouding her face unnerved him. She was always a wall of confidence, not caring what anyone thought of her. Like fresh air personified next to all the stuffy, pompous idiots in the room. He crafted a response part in truth and part to vex her. "I wouldn't have to pretend. Who wouldn't like a little pixie?"

She cast her eyes to the ceiling in exasperation. "I forget, there is no end to your flirtations."

He did tend to flirt with her when they were together. He had found it the best technique to disarm her and send her squirming. It was the most satisfying sensation.

She folded her arms across her chest. "Just be yourself and we shouldn't have a problem."

"Ah, but can you manage to be convincing in your affection for me?" Now this he would happily sign up for.

"I don't have to pretend anything. I only have to tolerate you enough for Ruth to feel comfortable in your presence."

He chuckled. "Ah, but what about Mr. Dobson?" He expected that was the real reason behind her willingness to aid him. "If you don't do a little pretending on your own, he might continue his pursuit and make a mess of everything." He could see in her eyes the moment his point landed. Mr. Dobson was a singular man and not at all right for the woman across from him. If they were going to strike a deal, they might as well be thorough.

"I despise that man," she grumbled.

"I know."

She stole a glance at his sister. "Can I at least tell Bridget that it's an act?"

"If you do, she will only question why, and then what will you say?"

Her gaze flicked to Bridget again. "I cannot deceive her."

"I don't expect you to. Just remember your promise to me."

She nibbled at the corner of her lip. "I suppose I can think of something."

"All while you are convincing the rest of the world that Richard Graham has more merit than you've previously believed?"

She grimaced—not a promising start.

He hadn't much to show for his life up until this point, and she knew that all too well. But he hadn't known responsibility then. Father hadn't wanted his involvement. It was different now, and he was determined to never shirk his responsibility again. "Well?" he hedged. "Think of Mr. Dobson."

"Must I? Oh, so be it," she huffed. "From this point forward, I am enamored with you, Richard Graham."

"Enamored?" He liked the sound of that far more than he should have. He wouldn't hold back either. Grace had it coming for her. He grinned and pushed the abandoned cribbage board aside. "Now this I cannot miss."

Chapter 6

GRACE LEFT THE BREAKFAST room the next morning with a sense of relief. Ever since her agreement with Richard, she had felt a burden lifted from her shoulders. She would finally be free of Mr. Dobson. Whenever the slightest misgiving niggled its way into her mind, she chased it away. It would take time to get used to the idea of Richard marrying Ruth, but surely with her sister's happiness, Grace would find contentment with the situation.

Nothing would go amiss. She wouldn't let it.

Mama met her in the corridor, standing on the black-and-white tiled floor, waving a note in the air. She had that excited look about her again—two days in a row.

"Mama?"

"It's from Mr. Graham," Mama said, coming to a stop in front of her. "He says their pond has frozen over, and he has invited us all over to skate on it."

"I am not overly adept at skating, but I suppose I could manage for Tobias's sake. He will surely enjoy the outing."

"A generous thought, Grace. But is not the invitation quite formal? What do you make of it?" She pointed to the words in the letter as she repeated them. "He specifically mentions the Misses Steeles and their family." When she looked up, her eyes were positively gleaming.

Grace opened her mouth, ready to make a snide remark about how Richard was finally making an effort to be a better brother by inviting entertainment and friends for his sister, but she remembered at the last moment that she was supposed to be fond of him. "We must thank him for his kindness."

Mama's brow rose. She knew Grace's frustration toward Graham better than most. "I will write to him and accept, of course, but it would be most appropriate for you to thank him in person as well."

"I will endeavor to do so as soon as we arrive." There. She had been perfectly cordial. This wasn't hard at all.

Mama's grin spread. "Wonderful. I shall tell the others of our change in plans for the day."

Not an hour later, they were all wrapped in fur cloaks and gloves, making their way to Belside's pond a small walk from the front of the house. A few trees and shrubs were covered in a lacy frost and the ground was stiff beneath their steps. A heavy cloud cover of gray reached every corner of the sky, making Grace wonder if it would snow again.

Bridget and Richard, bundled in warm outer clothes, were already gliding across the ice.

Tobias ran ahead to meet them, his boots crunching against the frozen grass.

"How long do we plan to stay?" Ruth asked their parents.

"Until we turn into icicles," Papa responded.

Grace couldn't help but smile at his excitement. Papa was not as strict or stoic as some fathers were. He enjoyed a good lark with the rest of them.

The Grahams had a crate full of skates next to a bench, and by the time the Steeles reached it, Tobias had already dug out a pair and had them laced to the bottom of his boots.

"Slow pokes," he said, hobbling on the blades to the pond's edge. "Catch me if you can." He stepped onto the ice with ease and sailed across its glassy surface.

Bridget and Richard stepped off the ice a moment later.

"It's even better than two years ago," Bridget said, coming up beside Grace and taking her arm.

Two years ago, Bridget had skated for two weeks straight. Grace had attempted to do the same but with far less success. Last year, no one had skated. The family had still been in mourning, and no one had cared to think about forms of amusement.

Richard came up on her other side but spoke to the group at large. "We are glad you all could join us. The ice is holding decently, but avoid the section under the willows. It's not as thick over there."

Mama tapped Papa's arm. "Lace up quickly, dear, so you can catch Tobias and tell him to avoid the willows."

Grace dug out a pair of wooden skates for herself, carefully avoiding the metal blade she knew had likely been sharpened just that morning. Ruth was next to finish her skates and stepped slowly to the pond's edge.

"Let me help," Richard said to Ruth, extending his arm.

Curious, Grace watched as Ruth's arm rigidly accepted Richard's. They looked hesitantly at each other before Ruth released him and made her way onto the ice alone.

Something about the interaction rankled her, and she struggled to know why. Perhaps she didn't like watching someone else's relationship beginning, or perhaps the two were so opposite she couldn't imagine them fitting together. Or maybe it ran deeper—a reflection of her own worry that such a relationship would never happen for her. She turned to lace her skate, but Mama caught her eyes.

"Interesting," she whispered.

"I don't know what you could mean," Grace hissed, reaching for her second skate. Why was she annoyed? Richard and Ruth were supposed to be warming to each other. *This was the plan.* Why did she feel jealous? She could admit Richard was attractive, but it took more than appearance for her to be won over. And Richard's lackadaisical approach to life in his adolescence had perpetuated in his adulthood. From what she'd heard, he hadn't taken his studies seriously or spent a single second thinking about his future. He'd opted to stay with friends instead of returning for the summer, visiting only on occasion. Certainly he was home now, but his presence hadn't changed his attitude. Family was not his highest priority, and she would never be more than a gnat in his ear—just the way she liked it.

"Hurry," Bridget prompted. "We can practice our turns together."

"I've never been good at turns," she reminded. "Slow and steady is my preference, remember?"

"A practical approach," Richard said, returning to them. "I will take Miss Steele's arm while she warms up, Bridget. We wouldn't want her hurting herself before she remembers how to skate."

He was goading her, and she wanted to volley with a remark about how she was not in need of any practice. Unfortunately, Richard likely knew the truth about her lack of skills, and there was no use pretending.

"That is a magnificent idea," Bridget answered. "Don't you dare complain, Grace. I want you to skate with me for the entire afternoon."

When Grace reluctantly met Richard's gaze, he winked. Her eyes widened. This wasn't him being helpful. This was him being *crafty*. Knowing she was playing a part was much easier than admitting to her weakness on the ice. She could play along. "Who am I to argue with magnificence?" She exaggerated the word for Richard's sake, barely holding back the sarcasm. Let his ego eat up her kindness while he could. It wouldn't be forever. She had hoped to warm up on Papa's arm, but this was the perfect opportunity to hatch their plan. She looped her arm through Richard's with far more confidence than her sister had.

"Enjoy yourself, darling," Mama said.

Grace did not respond. That woman didn't care which of her daughters had Richard Graham's attention so long as one of them kept it forever. In a few weeks' time, Ruth would make Mama very happy.

Grace set her first foot on the ice, and it nearly went out from under her. She barely held back her shriek.

"Careful," Richard said, steadying her.

It was one thing to embarrass herself in front of Bridget, but in front of Richard it was mortifying. "Thank you," she muttered.

"After a few times around, you'll find your footing."

She didn't care to be the worst at something. "Tobias and Ruth had made it look so easy. Are you sure my skates aren't sharper than theirs and a tad more dangerous?"

He laughed. "It could be a possibility. A very small one."

Bridget rushed by her like she had been born to skate, turning in a full circle without disrupting her balance. Ruth and Tobias were lining up for a race.

Grace followed Richard's eyes to where they stood. "What's your plan?"

He looked down at her. "Skate with you around the pond."

"I mean, after that. You had a dual purpose for inviting us here, did you not?"

"I confess I did."

"It was a good idea, but now what?"

He squinted at her. "I thought I would leave that up to you. Scheming is, after all, your specialty, not mine." He pulled her more fully onto the ice.

Her brow furrowed. "I am choosing not to take offense to that veiled insult since I am supposed to be thinking of your finer qualities, whatever they may be."

"I will happily list them for you, if it helps."

That could take all day. She shook her head, her feet doing their best to keep up with his. "Don't change the subject. Is it safe to assume that you did not come up with a plan and that you are hoping I will take it from here?"

He gave a shoulder shrug. "I am new to faking courtships with women. Perhaps you have some experience you might lend me?"

She gave him a very dull stare, which was quite brave of her since she really should have been watching her skates.

"No? Well then, I suppose we will have to forge our way one step at a time."

She risked falling again and narrowed her eyes at him, her skates wavering as she did. "You'd better not take your flirtations too far."

He set his free hand on top of hers to steady her again. "You'd better not forget you like me and say something rude."

She emitted a nervous laugh, very aware of the strange pressure and warmth seeping through her mitten. "Touché."

"Ah, I made you laugh. An improvement. We are well on our way to fooling everyone."

She shook her head. "The only one you're fooling right now is yourself. Can anyone truly believe the two of us could make a match?" She was proficient in chasing away men, and he had a trail of swooning women on his heels. Two such repelling opposites had no business being together.

"It appears we are fooling your parents. I caught your mother watching us as we skated off together. It made me worry that my acting skills are too good."

Mama was a gullible target. She believed her daughters were capable of ensnaring hordes of the finest suitors. She was destined for disappointment. "Your surprise visit yesterday has already gone to her head. Instead of wondering about your sudden interest, she has immediately jumped to matrimonial conclusions. She has no preference which daughter you pick, so that is in your favor."

Grace watched Tobias easily beat Ruth in their race, and Bridget rushed to join them for a second run.

"You will be happy to know that you chose the better skater for your real relationship," she added, admiring Ruth's elegant form.

Richard chuckled. "Where is the fun in that? I'd much prefer to have a woman by my side than chase after her." Grace knew she shouldn't react, but her stomach tightened. He seemed to realize what he'd said and cleared his throat. "I mean, I hope I do not have to chase Ruth for long."

A disobedient foot slid slideways, and she instinctively leaned into Richard. In some rather quick maneuvering, he managed to switch the arm that held hers and threw his free arm around her waist.

Her waist!

She blinked up at his light-blue eyes and his much too satisfied grin.

"Another time around?" he asked, his smile widening.

Oh, he was good at this. "Don't gloat," she said, carefully extricating herself from his arms. Her heart pounded much too fast for a little stumble.

"I'm not gloating. It's just nice seeing there is something you don't excel at."

"This is one of many things, but it won't keep me from trying." She pushed away from him. She'd felt a little thrill from Richard before on an occasion or two, and it scared her then as much as it did now. She was doing well enough, and a few falls wouldn't kill her. Staying on Richard's arm might though. He was too convinced of his own self-importance, and she needed to remember how very much she disliked him.

"What about our planning session?" he argued after her.

She shook her head. "A woman doesn't plan how a man will court her. You will have to put some effort into it."

He didn't have to skate fast to catch her; in fact, he had to slow down. "And what of your end of the deal?"

"I won't disappoint you, Richie dear," she said with a cheeky grin. "No one outside your family loves Belside manor more than me. But I can only take courtship in small doses, and I am afraid I have reached my fill for the day."

She had almost said she had reached her fill of *him*, but that wouldn't have been nice. And she was trying to be on her best behavior. She liked loathing Richard, and she didn't want anything to interfere with that.

Most especially Richard himself.

Chapter 7

RICHARD WASN'T USED TO drinking melted chocolate with short-bread, and especially not in the middle of the day. They'd taken Sunday off skating but had gathered again this morning for a second day of diversion on the ice. Afterward, Grace and Bridget announced their refreshment of choice and dragged them all into the drawing room. Only Mr. and Mrs. Steele had escaped, claiming business at home.

"A simple serving of tea and scones was not good enough for you?" He teased the women warming themselves in front of Belside's over-sized fireplace.

"The ordinary will never suffice for us," Bridget said. "Besides, there is nothing better than Aunt Edith's shortbread recipe. It should be famous."

"I agree, and who would want tea when they can have chocolate?" Grace shook her head like he was mad.

He was about to say himself, but he hadn't had melted chocolate in some time and could drink it without complaining. Relaxing back in a cushioned elbow chair, he took a sip. The dark liquid warmed his throat and middle. It was less bitter than the last time he had had it. In fact, he rather enjoyed it.

Bridget must have been watching him. "Grace requested it served with extra sugar and cream. What do you think?"

He took another sip. "Is that cinnamon?"

Grace nodded. "And just a hint of vanilla. Your cook has perfected our family recipe." She took a sip, tipped back her head, and sighed. "They had better have this in heaven."

Her over-the-top response was amusing. "I admit it's the best melted chocolate I've ever had."

A maid came in with a stack of quilts Bridget had asked for. He set his cup down and hurried to take the load. He passed one to Ruth, who avoided his gaze. Next was Bridget, who forgot to thank him. And Grace—when she accepted hers—met his gaze, thanked him, and almost smiled.

He thought about their reactions all the way back to his seat where he picked up his plate. He bit into his toast and chewed on his thoughts. After two different days of skating for a few hours each with the Steele family, Richard wasn't any closer to knowing Ruth better. Mr. and Mrs. Steele had to have had their suspicions about his intentions, but so far Grace had made it difficult for him to show any real partiality toward her. A few times around the pond on his arm, and then she was glued to Bridget's side. Perhaps he shouldn't have balked at inheriting a horse farm like his cousin Alden after all. He was officially failing at courting two different women. He had thought himself charming enough, but he could not even manage a fake courtship. At least Ruth had stayed for refreshment. That had to count for something.

And Grace? She was a complex puzzle with different sides she did not always show to people. But she had encouraged him to put in a little effort, and he wasn't going to shirk a challenge. There was no better place to start than in the privacy of his own home. That way if he bumbled anything, the rest of society need not witness it.

"How about a game?" he asked, prodding Grace's attention with the suggestion.

It was his sister who answered for her. "Oh, yes," Bridget said, her cheeks blooming into a smile. "What do you have in mind?"

"I was thinking of a word game."

"Tiles?" Tobias asked.

"The very one. I believe we have a set in the box on the mantel." He moved to retrieve it.

"I think I will walk home," Ruth announced suddenly.

Grace's gaze darted from her sister to Richard and back again. "But you adore word games."

He lifted the box with one hand and turned toward Ruth. "I am most reluctant to have you walk in this cold. Let me prepare my carriage for you. I must insist."

"Very well." Ruth settled back in her seat.

He swallowed. "While we wait, perhaps you can join us for one round of tiles?"

Her eyes darted to the door and back to him. "I suppose."

He handed the game to Tobias to prepare on the tea table while he sent a footman to the stables. When he returned, the faint smell of chocolate still lingered in the air. The others were gathered around the table, Grace and Bridget sitting on the carmine Turkish rug with their blankets on their laps, Ruth perched on the edge of the sofa, and Tobias on his knees. No other group would be able to relax so fully together. But it was more than that. His family was not so comfortable together since Father died. This felt like a glimpse from better days.

"What letter game did we decide on?" He pulled his chair up and positioned himself next to Grace. She eyed him warily, but he only smiled at her and rummaged through the off-white tiles. "Anagrams?"

"Please, no," Tobias whined. "It is impossible to beat my sisters. Play scramble. If you cannot decipher your word in sixty seconds, you're out."

"Very well." Pulling a few toward him, he selected the letters he needed. While still jumbled, he pushed them toward Tobias.

They all began counting the seconds out loud, but he sorted it with ease. "Done. Skating."

"He always goes easy on the first round," Bridget explained. "Don't get too comfortable."

He glanced up at her. She remembered? They hadn't played this since . . . since before Father. A wave of guilt coursed through him. Should he have spent more time with her? It hadn't been easy seeing to the estate and managing Mother's emotions. He reassured himself once more that she had Grace. She didn't need his attention too.

Grace selected the next set of tiles. Bridget studied the letters, tapping her chin with her finger while their counting neared sixty seconds. "Oh! Perfume."

Grace laughed. "Did the letter P give it away?"

Bridget nodded. "I know how you love a good fragrance."

Richard's brow quirked. He hadn't known this about her. Is that why she always smelled wonderful? Her scent was never overpowering but more like a soft, delicate flower. He was tempted to lean toward her so he might better describe it to himself, but the movement of tiles reminded him to focus on the game before him. He had more important matters to pay attention to than discerning scents.

Bridget took a turn, then Tobias, and finally Ruth. Ruth's word was simple: music. She did not seem wholly invested in the game. Was it so hard to be away from home? Or was it his company? Or the game?

Soon enough it was Richard's turn again. Time to add a little spice to this round. With one finger he pulled tile after tile toward him. Once he had a decent pile, he slid them in front of Grace.

She gave him a questioning look.

This was going to be fun.

Her fingers moved the pieces, lining them quickly like little tin soldiers. This was not a challenging word. It was a strategic move. He started off the counting himself. He set his hand on his chin, hovering much too close.

He knew the moment she saw the word. Her eyes widened slightly, and the softest pink began to fill her cheeks. Was . . . was she blushing?

"Adoration?"

She said the word carefully, as if not trusting it. More pink settled on her face. It didn't look like the flush of anger that their interactions tended to bring out. Had he embarrassed her?

"Interesting choice, brother," Bridget said slowly.

Tobias snickered. "I'd say. But it's just a silly game. He cannot really admire her. It's Grace, after all. She drives men away with her smart words and glares."

Grace's blush faded in an instant.

Richard frowned at the lad. "Apologize at once, Tobias. Your sister deserves your respect."

Tobias's face turned sheepish. Richard knew the lad looked up to him, and he hoped he'd take his words to heart.

"Sorry, Grace," Tobias muttered. "I shouldn't have said that."

Richard glanced down at Grace, who for once, seemed without a ready response.

She cleared her throat. "You are forgiven." She jumbled his tiles together as if they had never existed and gathered some of her own. She surprised him by sliding them his way.

He fully expected an insult.

OCIERH

He spotted an R for ridiculous, but there were not enough letters for that and too many to use the C for cad. What other insults might Gracie May fancy?

Seconds ticked by while he moved the letters around, his fingers stilling on the last tile. "Heroic?" He shifted the last tile into place. Sure enough, that was the word. He swung his eyes to Grace. Her bold gaze met his.

"Why, Miss Steele. How unexpectedly charitable of you," he said, his voice dropping a little lower than he intended.

She didn't bat an eyelash. "I do have my moments."

This was definitely one of them. Her eyes appeared more green than blue in this light, or was it more blue than green? Either way, they looked uncharacteristically lovely.

Her pert pink mouth settled into a challenging smile that no man had yet conquered, but surely dozens had tried. Not him, of course. He knew his boundaries. He swallowed and finally broke the strange connection between them. Perhaps this is why they were better off as sparring partners. Anything else felt unsettling.

Bridget went next. She slid her letters to Grace. Grace had always been quick at this game—or every game for that matter—but she hesitated as she lined up the last few letters. "The word is *confused.*"

His sister was another smart one, and she had caught the shift he and Grace were attempting to make. She didn't look angry, thank goodness, but no other emotion settled on her face. He would wager to guess she was still deciding what to make of them.

"I suppose I am next," Ruth announced. "The carriage should be readied now, so this will be my last turn." She gathered a few tiles and passed them to Bridget.

Bridget unscrambled the word and bent over it. "Courtship?"

Ruth stood. "Thank you for the skating and refreshments." She actually met Richard's eyes when she spoke. "Good day to you all."

"Wait for me," Tobias said, pulling himself off the floor. "This game is getting too personal for my taste."

"I will see you out," Bridget gave Richard and Grace a peculiar look and followed the others from the drawing room.

An awkward air settled between him and Grace. He scratched his chin and turned to her. "That went well."

She covered her mouth but the slight shake of her shoulders gave away her silent laugh.

"What's so humorous?"

She shook her head. "Nothing."

"What?"

"The poor souls. They actually believe that you . . . that we . . ." her laugh slipped out. "I'm sorry. It's unfathomable."

Why didn't he think it was funny? Granted, he wasn't proud of deceiving anyone, least of all his sister and neighbors. But why did she persist in thinking the worst of him? What was so wrong with her liking him? He could see himself liking her. Maybe. If he tried. He shook his head, refusing to finish the thought.

"What is it? You look in poor humor all of the sudden."

"I'm never in poor humor. I do not get upset easily."

She leaned against the tea table. "You're right. If there is something worth admiring about you, it's probably that. But how do you explain that frown of irritation?"

His forced smile came readily after a year and more of practice and he gave her an indirect response. "You have not taken me up on it before, but if you recall, I have offered plenty of times to list some of my finer attributes for you to acquaint yourself with. I can never understand these frequent occasions where you seem to struggle to grasp my good qualities while everyone else has no trouble in discovering them with ease."

She tapped her lips in simple mockery. "And yet you fail to understand that in making such a list, you are demonstrating your sense of self-importance that I continually disdain."

"You two," Bridget shook her head from the doorway. "The minute I think there is a truce between you, I am proved wrong. That game—never mind the particulars—is proof it is possible. Do try, for my sake. It can be most difficult living with you both."

"I don't live here," Grace said, the same time he said, "She doesn't live here."

Bridget huffed. "I suppose not, but Grace is as much a sister to me and is welcome anywhere I am. And my brother, obviously, owns this house, so the two of you need to learn to get along."

No one had more patience for his and Grace's bickering than Bridget, but it seemed she had met her limit.

"Bridget," Grace began.

"I know," Bridget said, holding up her hand, "you think it impossible. But a sudden idea has come to my head."

"Go ahead," Richard prompted.

"We are going to spend more time in each other's company."

Instinctively, Richard looked at Grace, whose gaze swung to meet his. How incredibly fortuitous of his sister.

"I agree," he said, slapping his knee. "I have been focusing far too much on the estate. With the holiday nearly upon us, there is no reason I cannot step back and be with my family."

"I'm not family," Grace said from beside him.

He set his forearms on his thighs and leaned toward her, lowering his voice for her to hear. "Yet," he said.

She pressed her lips together and whispered. "Is it inevitable?"

"Very." Her much too sea blue eyes widened, and he took a moment to appreciate them. Maybe his children would be lucky enough to inherit their aunt's features. But if they did, they'd better put a little more softness behind their gazes. He knew exactly what Grace thought of him, and it had nothing to do with flattering thoughts about his own eyes.

"Enough," Bridget said, coming into the room. "It has been decided and neither of you can talk me out of it.

Richard cleared his throat. "Miss Steele might not be supportive, but your brother will not disappoint you." He grinned a little at Gracie's wicked glare. "I think it has been too long since we have had the Steeles over for dinner."

"Yes!" Bridget squealed and clapped.

"Saturday night. What do you say, Miss Steele? You cannot disappoint us."

"Oh?" she said. "You won't be able to bear it?"

He set a hand to his heart. "I will be thoroughly crushed."

She fought her smile, which he decided then and there was his favorite look of hers. It was this battle between her resisting reacting to him and him getting to her. One day he would get to her fully and prove that he was more of a man than she thought him to be. With that realization, she would willingly smile at him without a single trace of artifice. Such a moment would be incredibly satisfying.

Until then, he would be forced to depend on his charm—the only blasted skill he seemed to possess. First, woo Grace, and then woo Ruth. But he would also seek an alternative route in case he failed. He would ask his solicitor to search for an investment opportunity with a quick turnaround. While this was as unlikely as earning Aunt's money with his marriage, he would exhaust every avenue.

Chapter 8

GRACE NODDED ABSENTLY WHILE Mr. Dobson prattled on and on about buttons. From the corner of the room, Ruth plunked at the pianoforte as if the tune were as bored as the conversation. Grace's thoughts wandered to Bridget's note. It had been sent over just before Mr. Dobson arrived and had included menu options for their joint family dinner at the end of the week. Sweet Bridget. She couldn't stop talking about the event.

Grace believed it was Richard's voluntary participation that had Bridget so ecstatic. With just the Steeles invited, it was hardly worth getting excited about. Her brother, on the other hand, had neglected her entirely too much this past year, and the poor thing was starved for his attention.

Mr. Dobson's voice lifted a single notch, catching her attention. "The Spaniards used to hide potent and dangerous substances in their buttons to smuggle them across the seas."

Now that was quite an interesting fact. But Mr. Dobson quickly returned to noting the differences within his personal button collection, and she drifted back to thinking about Bridget. Had she deceived her dearest friend by not explaining the real reason behind the dinner party? But how could she disappoint her? Not to mention, telling Bridget about her brother's plans of courtship would make it incredibly difficult to leave out the part about her estate being in trouble. It was better not to say anything until she had to.

"Yes," she said with a nod to Mr. Dobson, but she was really talking and nodding to herself.

Speaking of resolutions to herself, she intended to see some results from her and Richard's bargain. It had been *three* days since their game of tiles, and Grace hadn't seen any sign of the odious man. Which meant she had been forced to suffer through two separate visits from Mr. Dobson.

This second one was trying her patience to an unholy degree.

Thinking of the first was slightly easier. Though thoughts of Richard courting her at all made her scowl deeply at the carpet. His words would be all honey and sweetness but full of empty meaning. They'd confuse her and try to shake her resolve against him. She had to be strong, for even the impenetrable walls of Jericho were brought down by words.

"Miss Steele, are you listening?"

She pulled her gaze up from the floor, smoothing her expression. Admittedly, she had not heard every word, but she could easily repeat the history of the button, should anyone inquire. She could also relay how many buttons Mr. Dobson was in possession of. Three-hundred forty-six, to be precise. He had acquired six new buttons just this week. "Mr. Dobson, even if I tried not to listen, how could I prevent it?" She said it as sweetly as she could, and sure enough, he entirely missed her point, his droning picking up right where he left off.

How perfectly . . . annoying.

Richard. Richard. Richard. She ground out his name in her head. Was he planning on courting her, or had he decided that he would have better luck praying somewhere for a miracle? Either way, she would curse his name before she heard another sentence about buttons.

The drawing room door filled with a dark shadow, and she looked up. "Richard!" She leaped to her feet. She hadn't meant to shout his name—especially not his given one—but she had been repeating it in her head at the very moment she saw him.

"Happy to see me?" He grinned at her.

She punctuated each word of her response. "You have no idea."

He laughed, gave a short bow, and strolled into the room as if it was his house. "Mr. Dobson, old boy. Good to see you."

"What a greeting. I'm only twenty-six," Mr. Dobson said. "What estimation do you use for naming ages?"

Richard's smile faltered. "Old is relative. I meant it as a term of familiarity. Speaking of familiarity, I see you have been spending too much time at the Steeles again."

Mr. Dobson's face soured. "I believe I have as much right as you do to be here."

"I wouldn't be so confident." Richard nodded to Ruth, whose fingers had stilled on the piano. "Don't let me stop you, Miss Steele. Your music is exceptional."

Ruth pulled a soft melody from the keys as her response. How did Richard have such an effect on people? It also begged the point that Grace should have practiced her music more. She could be the one hiding behind the ivory keys instead of sitting next to Mr. Dobson.

"Will you sit, Mr. Graham?" Grace asked. With the slightest nudge of her head, she motioned to the half cushion of space between her and Mr. Dobson.

Richard was no small man, and his brow slowly lifted.

She understood his concern, but it was hardly the time to consider his comfort. What about hers? He owed her after their time ice-skating. Hadn't she done her part well enough? She motioned again to the spot beside her, her eyes widening this time for emphasis.

He flashed a smile that nearly masked his hesitation. "Uh, I think I will sit, thank you. He came directly toward them. "Excuse me." And then without preamble, he tried to sit exactly where she wanted him—where he could block out Mr. Dobson from her view. His effort was worthy, although perhaps she had misjudged his abilities. He practically sat on one of her legs, and by the sound of Mr. Dobson's voice, he had done the same to his.

"Oof!" she groaned, shoving the large man. Worse than the burning in her leg from the sudden unsolicited touch, he smelled like he'd just walked off Mount Olympus carrying the musk of the gods with him. Heaven help her.

Mr. Dobson must have shifted because Richard moved over, giving her room to breathe normal air again. Her cheeks remained flushed with heat, and she discreetly batted her hand to cool them. Where was her fan when she needed it?

"This is comfortable." Richard's tone was absent of sarcasm, but his words were anything but.

"Hardly," Mr. Dobson grumbled.

Grace smoothed her dress, attempting to recover her composure, and then looked sideways at Richard. "You're late."

"Am I?"

She nodded, noting for the first time the fatigue lines around his eyes. Had he not been sleeping well? "Very late. By three days."

He coughed into his hand, doing a terrible job at hiding his amusement. "Miss Steele, it is a privilege to have you count the passage of time until you see me again. I deeply apologize for my prolonged absence from your side. It was a great sacrifice to keep myself away."

She smiled prettily at him. "I do appreciate your apology, but my forgiveness is not so easily won. I do hope you will endeavor to make up for your lapse in judgment." She looked pointedly past him to Mr. Dobson.

Richard turned to the man, which clearly took some effort to avoid their knees hitting and mostly consisted of a slight movement of his head and shoulders. "Is it just me or does courting a woman take more effort with each passing generation?"

"I am not old enough to know," Mr. Dobson said.

"Ah, perhaps it is my astute wisdom with such cases as these," he said. "But it is no matter. I am helpless when Miss Steele asks anything of me."

Her brow rose. "Oh? I shall endeavor to remember that."

"Surely you speak of Miss *Ruth* Steele," Mr. Dobson said, his voice growing thin.

Richard scratched the back of his head. "Ah, I can see how you might have been mistaken. Were it not uncouth to discuss such personal details of preference with the ladies present, I would endeavor to explain."

Mr. Dobson's frustration seemed to be climbing at the same rate as his breeches. Grace blinked twice and leaned forward slightly. He was gripping the fabric at the knees and . . . yes, the buttons on the bottom of his breeches just above his boots were missing. They were probably the six new ones added to his collection.

"By all means," Mr. Dobson said, sticking his chin in the air. "Let us step into the corridor where we can have privacy."

"Now?" Richard asked.

Mr. Dobson gave a firm nod. "I see no reason to delay the discussion of preference, as my own should be made known to you forthwith."

Richard looked at her for help, but she pretended not to notice. But what was the phrase? He had made his bed and must lie in it? Yes, that was the one. Let him lie down, forthwith. And preferably before she started laughing.

"Very well." Richard stood and Mr. Dobson followed. She watched them leave the room before she sat back and sighed with satisfaction. Finally, Richard was proving his worth.

"Grace," Ruth hedged. "What in heaven's name is going on?"

Grace hadn't even noticed the music stop again. "I . . . don't know what you could mean."

"Grace," she hissed. "Are those two men fighting over you?"

"I certainly hope so."

Ruth groaned. "What if there is a duel?"

Grace squinted at the door. "Do you think we could be so fortunate?"

Ruth hit a low chord on the piano, her response unmistakable.

"Do not upset yourself. I doubt it will come to that." Grace waited for the gentlemen to return, but the minutes ticked by without them. Ruth's music turned into a jumble of tunes, a new one beginning before the last had ended.

Grace dusted off her hands and climbed out of her seat. Waiting had made her hungry, and she wanted to skip down to the kitchens and find something more satisfying than tea.

"Grace! You cannot leave me here alone. What if they come back?"

"I don't think they will at this point. But do not fret. Whatever has happened, I trust Richard."

Ruth's brow rose in the perfect mimic of Mama's. "You mean *Mr. Graham*?"

"Not you too. Mr. Graham was Richard's father. He will have to be just Richard."

Ruth hurried from the pianoforte to her side. "Then is he courting you?"

It sounded so impossible to even pretend an answer. "Maybe," she managed.

Ruth worried her lip. "Did he ask me on a walk the other day to be close to you?"

Grace found herself blinking rapidly again. "I—I cannot say."

Ruth heaved a sigh. "I am deeply relieved. I feared he might be interested in me. That would have been a true devastation, for I haven't the faintest attachment to him in return. There cannot be a worse pair, I assure you. Can you imagine? Me, married to a socialite?" She shivered.

Oh, dear. This was a problem. "At the very least he is handsome," Grace hedged.

Ruth grimaced. "If you do not mind his narrow jaw."

Grace balked. "Narrow? Romeo himself could not have had a finer jaw."

"That is your opinion, sister. His face is too expressive. And his voice carries."

Grace couldn't believe what she was hearing. "He is *confident*."

Ruth shook her head. "I call it loud."

Grace huffed. He was nothing of the sort. Why was Ruth finding fault with the best parts of him?

"I must prefer the brooding, serious type. So, you see, you are a much better fit for him than I." Ruth gave Grace a knowing look and vacated the room, leaving her alone to stare after her.

What? Her sister was wrong. Grace wasn't a better fit. Richard was fun to banter with and even more fun to rile, but this was just a game. It didn't matter how good he smelled or that he kept coming to her rescue—first at the ball, then with Tobias, and now with Mr. Dobson—none of that mattered. She still despised how conceited he was. And even if he was trying to salvage things with Bridget, it was too little too late.

This was silly. There was nothing to talk herself out of. Besides, Richard wanted *Ruth*. She rubbed the back of her neck. She had merely been trying to point out that he did have some good qualities amongst the bad ones. But Ruth had been so against him that it would be exceptionally hard to convince her to care for him. Indeed, it might be easier to convince Richard to find someone else altogether.

Dropping her hand to her side, she straightened. If Richard could remove Mr. Dobson, then it was her duty to persuade Ruth.

Fair was fair.

Chapter 9

RICHARD STOOD BESIDE BRIDGET, welcoming the Steele family into his home. He was tired, having rode home from a quick trip to Birmingham to meet with a potential investor. It had turned out to be an utter waste of his time. The day on horseback had left his muscles tight—muscles that had not recovered from helping a tenant family rebuild their home that had partially burned to the ground earlier that week.

He hadn't known what to do, but leaving three children and their parents out in the cold was not an option. He had worked alongside the builder and thatcher and a few other laborers, learning skills he had never even seen before. It had been gratifying when they had finished, but now neither time nor money were on his side. Unless he received a Christmas miracle and the perfect investment, marrying Ruth appeared to be his only option. He'd finally written to his friend to secure a special license from the archbishop. God willing, he would have a cooperative bride to go with it.

As if hearing his thoughts, Ruth approached him first, wearing a pale yellow satin gown that brought out the fairness in her features.

"Good evening, Miss Steele." He smiled and dipped his head. "Thank you for joining us."

She curtsied but said nothing.

He smothered his sigh before it could escape. He hoped his cousins were faring better than he was with their Twelfth Night matches. Apparently, his was still afraid of him. He looked beyond Ruth to her sister, who was stepping toward him. Grace's gown of choice was more bold. It consisted of a white bodice with a dark-purple overlay. But it was her eyes that arrested him. They were smiling at him in a knowing way that made him a little uneasy but captivated nonetheless.

"Miss Steele," he said, dipping his head. He held her eyes, framing a question with his own. "You look a picture this evening."

"I thank you for the compliment." She held his gaze a moment longer before turning to her sister. "Ruth, isn't Mr. Graham exceptionally kind?"

He tried not to appear surprised. Any time Grace said something nice about him it felt like a gigantic lie.

Ruth looked at him for a brief moment before answering her sister. "Mr. Graham is always kind."

"When he wants to be," Bridget interjected from beside him. "Tonight he is redeeming himself by playing host."

"Did I need redeeming?" he asked.

Grace was quick to nod. "Very much so."

Ruth frowned and Grace quickly shook her head as if she regretted her words. "I meant that we have not dined together for some time, and I am glad that it has been remedied."

Richard noticed Bridget's curious look, but Ruth's was what concerned him. She had a knowing look, like she saw right through her sister's intentions. Was that a good thing or bad?

He greeted Mr. and Mrs. Steele next. Mr. Steele set his arm on Richard's shoulder, his grip strong and his whiskered face happy. "It's good for our families to be spending so much time together, Graham."

"It is," Richard said, suddenly a little nervous. He held great respect for Mr. Steele, and he had the feeling that the man would welcome him as a son-in-law. The idea was still daunting to him. They visited for a few minutes before dinner was announced.

Bridget had done all the arranging, so once at the head of the table, he was surprised to find himself seated next to Mr. Steele and Mrs. Steele on one side of him and Grace on the other. Ruth was beside her and Bridget at the end. He could easily understand why Bridget had not placed herself beside him, but not her dearest friend?

Mr. and Mrs. Steele started discussing a painting of fruit on the wall that had been done by a neighbor years before.

"I thought you had died," Grace whispered, picking up her napkin.

He had almost missed her words. "Me?"

"In a duel. Shot by Mr. Dobson in an ignominious defeat." Her mouth barely moved, but this time he caught every unbelievable word.

Richard lifted his glass to his mouth and spoke quickly before taking a sip. "Mr. Dobson—kill me? You sorely underestimate me."

"Do I? Am I to understand that you killed Mr. Dobson then?"

He frowned, almost forgetting to be inconspicuous. "Why dirty my hands when a simple bribe would suffice?"

"Bribe?"

Mr. and Mrs. Steele took that opportunity to cease speaking, and everyone heard her.

Mrs. Steele's lips formed a stern line. "Grace, dear, why are you speaking of bribes at the dinner table?"

Grace grimaced. "Er—I was, uh . . ."

He jumped in to save her. "Miss Steele heard we were serving Blakewell pudding tonight and jokingly requested we serve it for the first course. The offered bribe was not made in earnest, I assure you."

Grace shot him a surprised but grateful look.

"Ah," Mrs. Steele said.

Mr. Steele chuckled. "My daughter takes after me. I admit, I have not had Blakewell pudding in some time and have quite the liking for it. I believe it is the flaky pastry base that makes it so delicious."

Bridget joined in. "My favorite is the layer of sieved jam."

"That is well enough," Mrs. Steele said. "But the filling made of egg and almond paste is what makes a Blakewell pudding so distinct."

Richard tucked his napkin in as the footmen set the first course on the table. "I am glad we are all anticipating Derbyshire's famous pudding." He winked at Grace when the others looked away. She had to admit that he had been the clever one this time.

Instead of smiling at him, she glared at him. What had he done wrong? It wasn't until the second course when he got a chance to discreetly ask her. "Don't tell me that one little wink from me has you flustered."

Unfortunately, the privacy at the dinner table was nonexistent, and she did not have a chance to answer him. Instead, she did something far more surprising.

"What a delightful meal," she suddenly announced. "Mr. Graham, I am delighted to see you did not fall asleep. Father, were you aware that Mr. Graham falls asleep the moment he is bored? It is a testament to our family that we have kept him awake."

Ah, she had caught the yawns he had tried to hide with his napkin. He wasn't embarrassed; in fact, he took her words as a challenge.

"Miss Steele is correct. It is her utterly charming company that has me so riveted tonight."

He met her shocked gaze and grinned.

"I have always thought both my daughters quite charming," Mr. Steele said. "I am pleased somcone finally noticed."

When Grace's eyes widened even further, he nearly choked on a bite of potatoes to keep from laughing. She must not have liked her father's emphasis on the word *finally*.

"Mr. Graham is too kind," Grace said. "But he is admittedly slow to see a prize when it is right in front of his nose. I am happy to hear he is *finally* catching on."

Bridget coughed into her shoulder.

Richard caught Grace's wild gaze again and held it, daring her to say something more. While he was eager to progress his plans with Ruth by pretending to court Grace, she would soon have them engaged if she persisted in her flirtations—albeit laced with hidden sarcasm. Perhaps he should not have risen to the occasion himself. He didn't dare look at either of her parents to guess at their thoughts.

After the pudding was served and gushed over, the women dismissed themselves to the drawing room. Port was set on the table, and he insisted Mr. Steele serve himself first.

"I appreciate your insights on crop rotation," Richard said, eager for some conversation that might clear the air between them. "My fields are looking a far sight better than last summer."

Mr. Steele gave a quick nod. "I would never fault your father, but your land steward was too old and too set in his ways. I am glad you have set him out to pasture and hired a fresh hand."

"Indeed, I am confident in Mr. Guiss's skills." Unfortunately, no matter the size of their harvest, it would not be sufficient to turn the fate of Belside.

"You are coming into your own, Graham. It is not an easy thing to step into your father's place like you did. Hard things have a way of turning a boy into a man, and I have seen you become one this last year. If I am not wrong, you are looking for a mistress of Belside next."

He swallowed, swirling the amber liquid in his glass. "I do hope to take a wife soon."

Mr. Steele nodded again, his arms folding over his chest. "It seems my Grace has caught your eye."

Blast. This wasn't happening. If he admitted his partiality to Grace, how would he later explain the transfer of his feelings to Ruth? It had sounded so simple coming from Grace, but the reality was far more complicated.

This was all her fault. The vexing minx had lured him into sparring again. And while he generally preferred such an activity with a practice sword and a fencing partner, these days, it was his verbal matches with Grace that fed his appetite. It was far better than thinking of the mess of his estate. But instead of passing insults and harmless flirtations, he should have been more wary of his new *business* partner.

She was far too clever for him.

"Grace would be a catch for any man," he finally managed to say. There. He'd been both honest and vague.

"She has practically grown up in this house. No woman would transition better. Indeed, it would feel more natural to both your mother and sister than any other choice you could make. They already look at her as family. I am surprised I did not think of the match myself."

Nor he. The room swelled with an abominable heat, and he pulled at his choking cravat. Dare he mention how they would never get on? How his aunt would withhold necessary funds if he dared even try it?

"Did I speak too soon?" Mr. Steele asked. "I can see I have made you uncomfortable. That was the farthest from my intention."

"Not at all," Richard lied. "I have not yet settled my mind on my future. It is too early to tell—certain things."

Mr. Steele chuckled. "Courtship is not for the faint of heart. And if I dare add, especially if Grace is involved."

Richard gripped his thighs under the table. "Thank you for understanding."

"I was once in your place. Courting Mrs. Steele was an adventure."

"I am not against adventures, but there are other matters . . ." his voice trailed off.

Mr. Steele nodded. "I know you are uneasy about your estate. I cannot profess to know all the particulars, but it is admirable how you have reached out to the land owners around you and sought their advice. I have no doubt you will have this place turned around in no time at all."

Richard had come to him several times seeking guidance and instruction on running an estate, and his advice had been a godsend. But saving his estate was nothing hard work could change. He needed a miracle. He needed Aunt's money.

Mr. Steele pushed back his chair. "Come, let's not keep the ladies waiting any longer." The knowing look he gave Richard sent a wave of nausea through him.

Richard stood and obediently followed. Even though he had walked this short path between rooms a million times over, never had his feet dragged so. What sort of trap had he set for himself?

Chapter 10

GRACE HAD ACCOMPLISHED WHAT she had set out to do, but never had one of her successes left so many conflicting feelings. It had been three days since the dinner party, and her parents had been impossible to live with. Father kept sending her pleased looks and telling her how proud he was of her. Mama had found ways to slide the topic of weddings into every other conversation. Tuesday morning, she was in a particularly expressive mood. She was sure to mention her opinion of the best wedding dates, where to shop for fine but affordable wedding clothes, and an exhaustive menu of what to serve at wedding breakfasts.

The anxiety in Grace's middle soared toward her chest until every muscle strung tight. Mama's discussion of items to add to Grace's trousseau snapped her barely held patience. Grace set down her teacup with a clatter that seemed to rattle the entire drawing room. Ruth and Mama looked up expectedly at her from their needlework. Grace's own sewing was a complete mess. Every knot she had made in her embroidery had to be pulled out and fixed.

With no explanation for her shamble of nerves, she hurriedly faced the door. "I . . . I wonder why Mr. Dobson does not come to visit."

She swallowed back stomach bile. It had come to this. She would rather discuss the safe but dreadfully boring topic of buttons than plan a fictitious wedding to Richard Graham.

"I don't believe we will see much of Mr. Dobson in the future," Ruth said, her eyes dancing.

Grace frowned. "What do you mean?" She needed Mr. Dobson. No one else could lull her mind into such emptiness as he did. There was not a chance of any guilt or anxiety outside of ridding herself of him. How had she not appreciated how useful that man had been?

Ruth picked a thread from her gown. "Bridget told me at the party."

"Told you what?" Mama asked, leaning forward.

Grace instinctively did the same.

"Do you recall last Wednesday when both Mr. Graham and Mr. Dobson visited us?"

"Yes, I remember."

"Bridget was walking to our house when she stumbled upon them."

Grace shook her head. "I don't understand. We never had a visit from her that day."

"That is because after hearing the men's private conversation, she returned home so as not to be caught by her brother. You see, Mr. Graham told Mr. Dobson that there was mutual affection between himself and you and that Mr. Dobson ought to cry off before he was wounded by the situation."

Grace gasped. "He didn't!"

Ruth grinned. Never had her sister been so happy to discuss gossip before. "It was better than any novel I have ever read. I do believe Mr. Graham is smitten by you."

"I knew it!" Mama cried, clapping her hands.

"Bridget must have misheard." Grace shook her head fervently. "Ruth, you must know, I have heard him speak well of *you*. So, you see, he is confused and does not know his own mind."

"Then you must unconfuse him," Ruth said. "I have told you before; I am not his equal in personality."

Grace groaned, slouching back into the sofa. She was supposed to be pretending to like the man, but in a little more than a week's time, they had skipped from courtship to wedding planning. Just yesterday, she had made a detailed list of places to visit in London to help maintain her focus on the prize, but at the moment, not one of those places seemed worth this much trouble.

"Sit up," Mama said. "This is nothing to pout about. It's something to celebrate."

Celebrate? Grace whipped her head up. "Mama, you cannot make any insinuations. There is no understanding between us. All this wedding talk must cease." She wasn't about to engage herself to Richard Graham for the name of a favor. *That* was going too far.

Mr. Reed stuck his head in the door. "Pardon me, but Mr. Graham is here to pay a call."

Mama looked positively gleeful. "Hand me your sewing things, girls. Here, put them in this basket." She waved her hand to Mr. Reed. "We're ready now. Send him right in." She dropped her gaze to Grace. "Be on your best behavior and maybe this understanding we desire will come sooner than later."

They all stood as Richard entered the room. In his arms was a colorful bouquet of flowers. He must have sent for them from the hothouses a town over. Their loveliness exceeded any she had seen. His bow was like a flourish—masculine but with finesse. Drat that perfect man. He straightened and grinned, most particularly at her.

"Good morning, ladies. I have brought flowers for your table. I trust you had an excellent weekend?"

And he was far too happy for her taste. Had he not an inkling of what he had walked into?

"A very good weekend, Mr. Graham," Mama said. "You must sit and take tea with us." She pointed at the cushion beside Grace.

"I would like nothing better, but I have my phaeton hitched up outside. I remembered how much Miss Grace enjoys the conveyance. I thought I would offer to take her on a short excursion around our two estates before I return home. I have my groom with me and hot bricks and blankets."

Ruth smiled. "You have thought of the exact ways to please my sister." She stood and took the flowers from Richard. "I will see these find a proper place of honor."

Yes, Ruth *smiled*. At Richard. And she had spoken more than a dozen words. This was progress. If Ruth burying Grace in a bed of expectation could be seen as progress.

Grace didn't want to go on a carriage ride, even if she did love being in the open seats of a phaeton. If she accepted, it would be interpreted as an act of courtship—which would be a product of her own insane idea. If she declined, she would delay a chance to explain to Richard about the horrid turn of events that had come from their scheming. Either way, she was doomed.

She forced her mouth to move. "I shall fetch my cloak and mittens."

Not ten minutes later, dressed as warmly as was fashionably acceptable, she walked with Richard from the house to the long drive. His phaeton gleamed in the winter sun—the black a stark contrast to the muted browns of the grass and leafless trees beyond it. Small clumps of snow spotted the rest of the grounds.

When they reached the phaeton, Richard spoke first. "I had hoped to come yesterday, but I have tasked my solicitor with combing the countryside for investment opportunities with a quick turnaround. I traveled again yesterday to look into it. Sadly, it was as terrible as the one I learned about last week." He glanced at her once and then a second time. "You're rather quiet today."

Grace produced a single nod. "I'm thinking."

"Oh?" he said. "Should I be wary of some future ploy?"

She pulled at her mittens. "Not yet."

"Good, then dare I ask the subject of your thoughts?"

She gave a single shrug. She wouldn't mention how excited she was to smell the perfumes of each bloom he had brought. Thankfully, she had enough thoughts whirling through her mind to think of another to mention. "I am thinking of how you rid me of Mr. Dobson."

"I told you. I bribed him."

"But how?" He hadn't any money to spare.

He gave a crooked smile. "I gave him buttons."

That was not what she expected him to say. "Buttons?"

"Yes. There is a chest of gowns in my attic. Grandmother left behind several polonaise-style dresses with silk buttons. I simply had them removed and sent them over to him."

She gasped. "You ruined those beautiful gowns? It would have been better if you would have dueled him."

He laughed, loud and rich. "I will remember that next time." He stepped closer to the conveyance, but she stayed frozen in place.

"Did you say anything else to him?"

He frowned, his gaze drifting off as if he were thinking. "I am sure I did, but I cannot recall the exact words. I rode to Birmingham the very next morning and my weekend was just as busy. I think I said something to the effect that we were passionately in love and that he didn't stand a chance."

Grace's mouth dropped open. How did he so easily say those words, "passionately in love," without flinching. Good heavens. This was worse than what Bridget had overheard. "Richard—"

Before she could finish her sound verbal lashing, he set his hands on her waist and swooped her up into the air. Her arms flung to his shoulders as he transferred her like one would a feather to her seat high in the phaeton.

She released him to catch her breath, which came out shaky and unsettled. One would think he had embraced her by the way her heart stuttered in her chest. She quickly slid across the velvet seat to allow space between them. Richard climbed inside, and oblivious to her efforts to distance herself, he proceeded to cover her lap with a dense fur blanket. His motions were gentle and thorough, as he assured that not an inch of her lower half was exposed to the chilly air.

He was being much too kind.

"Go ahead, Briggs," he said to the groom, settling back into his seat. He turned to her, his face much too close to hers. "What was that you were saying earlier?"

He was employing this obnoxious behavior on purpose. He wanted her to react, but she was on to him. "I was about to declare how utterly stupid you are."

His sigh was more of content than the depressed state she wished to inflict. "Oh, good. You aren't mad."

She gave a short laugh, despite herself. "No, just annoyed."

He chuckled. "No one sees my weaknesses like you do, Gracie May. In fact, I sense you enjoy exploiting them."

"I *do* see them quite plainly. Call it a gift."

He chuckled again. "I cannot imagine why you despise me, but perhaps this is as good a time as any to discover why."

The last three days had upset her enough to tell him every word of how she'd felt for the entire last year. She opened her mouth to unload her thoughts, but he held up a hand to stop her.

"Uh, uh, uh. Let's remember that I did rid you of Mr. Dobson as promised. You must do your best to temper your words. I can be sensitive, you know."

"Ha! You have never taken offense to any of my words."

"That is because I find your insults so entertaining." His sly, flirtatious grin set her heart pounding.

She hated when that happened. Hated him for making it happen. If he meant anything by them, she could be flattered, but she knew he intended the opposite. "Besides the fact that *you* are *you*, and that in and of itself is terribly obnoxious, my frustration with you has doubled exponentially since your return from Oxford."

"From Oxford?" His brow puckered. "Does my presence keep you and Bridget from your escapades?"

"No one could manage that," she said. "It is your *utter* failure at being a good brother to Bridget during her time of need."

His jovialness disappeared in one cold instant. "What do you mean?"

Now that she said it, a sliver of guilt nagged at her middle. But she was justified, and shouldn't feel bad. "I mean that you neglected Bridget, and her suffering has been my own."

"Is that what she thinks? That I abandoned her?"

The hurt on his face was much stronger than she imagined it would be, and though she expected such a look of contrition would bring her a measure of satisfaction, it didn't. "It is what we both think."

He sighed, his gaze facing forward. "I suppose I've been consumed with my own grief and worry about the estate. I've been so convinced that I could change Belside's fate—even seeking financial counsel and guidance on the particulars of running an estate from every intelligent man I know. Keeping Belside in the family feels like keeping Father's memory alive. I've hardly been able to consider anything else since his death."

It was strange seeing Richard—a man she had thought pompous and nearly perfect—be vulnerable. It felt wrong, confusing, and everything in-between.

"I had no idea," she admitted a little begrudgingly. When she saw him with his friends, had he been trying to seek their advice? Had she misinterpreted the situation?

He adjusted the brim of his hat, pulling it lower. "Telling anyone the specifics would only garner pity, and pity won't save Belside."

There was no doubting the honesty and hints of embarrassment in his voice. She wasn't supposed to feel compassion for him, but his confession had punctured her anger and new emotions were seeping through. "It isn't right for anyone to suffer alone."

Not even him.

He studied her briefly, no doubt surprised she cared at all. "What if I deserve to suffer alone?"

The gruffness in his tone alarmed her. "H-how can you say that?"

He shrugged. "I suppose I have my reasons. One of which is my duty to my family. You can add poor brother and son to your list of my failings. I fooled myself into thinking that Bridget would manage well enough with you by her side, just as I imagined Mother's melancholy to fade after a few months' time."

She didn't want to add to any list. In fact, she wanted to rip the proverbial thing to shreds. All her anger had deflated, and she wanted to comfort him, to assure him that Belside would weather this crisis, that his mother would rally, and that Bridget would manage without him. But they would be false promises. She could ensure nothing. All these months she had harassed him, when underneath his cheerful facade was a stark layer of pain. Why had she not seen it?

"I tried my best to be there for your mother and sister." Grace's voice dropped to a whisper. "But they needed you. They still need you."

He frowned, heavy brows shadowing his almond eyes. Silence bounced between them like the cadence of the horses. It had been over a year, but sadness visited with every memory of Mr. Graham's death. A year and a half was not enough to erase the suffering he had unintentionally left in his wake.

Richard heaved a sigh. "Thank you for being honest with me, Gracie. My inadequacies have never been so prominent before, but I still needed to hear it."

No one was better at highlighting his failings than her, but didn't he realize how much he had to offer? "They love you, you know. Because of who you already are."

He sighed. "I wish that were enough."

"Do you really think it's not?"

He shrugged. "I suppose I do. There is too much I cannot control—the money, the house. It weighs on me."

Shame pricked her conscience so deeply she wanted to curl in on herself. "I'm sorry if my . . . my rudeness . . . added to your burdens."

"Nonsense. Sparring with you is the only entertainment I get these days." He forced a smile, but she saw through it this time. How often had his smiles been pretend?

"I will try to see that as a compliment."

"It is, Gracie, I promise. Your father knows a little of our situation, as does my solicitor, and a few friends I have reached out to for financial advice, but they do not know anything about my family. I prefer it that way. But you," he paused, his gaze studying her own, "you know it all."

The moment felt undeniably private, like he had opened a door and invited her in. He could have told any number of women about his problems. They certainly flocked after him when out in Society, but he was telling her instead. She knew it was because of her history with the family, but was there more to it? "Why do I have a feeling that no one really knows it all? Do you have anyone you confide in, Richard?"

"Not candidly like this, no. My friends are generally the fair-weather sort. I don't know if I have ever needed a confidante before. It feels refreshing to have some of this off my chest. I thank you for listening."

Daring not to speak for fear of breaking a spell his unguarded words had set on her, she ducked her head. She couldn't understand it—or him—but he needed a friend, and she suddenly wanted so dearly to be that person. She forced her head to lift again. "You don't have to keep thanking me. I want to listen."

"Do you?" He searched her gaze as if looking for more than just the answer to this question, and in doing so, set off a tingle of feeling through her limbs.

She felt sheepish, but she spoke the feelings on her mind anyway. "I know I have not been someone you could call a friend in the past, but I can be relied upon, should you need me."

"Not just because of the loyalty to my family?"

She thought carefully on her answer. "Perhaps initially, but I believe we can have a friendship of our own." And surprisingly, she meant it. Bridget would never believe it. *She* was having trouble believing it. It would take more curbing of her tongue, but she could try.

"I should like that," he said, ". . . to be friends."

She held his gaze before dipping a quick nod of agreement.

"Friendship has two ends to it," he said. "I will listen to your troubles as well."

"My troubles are nothing." She hastily dismissed her problems. They were not comparable to a threat on one's home.

"No matter the size or breadth, it doesn't matter to a true friend. Perhaps someday you can tell me why you want to go to London when I know you don't care a fig about the city itself."

She opened her mouth to tell him that she *did* like the city, but caught herself. If she meant what she had said about friendship, she had to trust Richard in return. "I do prefer the countryside. I only want to find a husband." As soon as the words left her mouth, she regretted them. She was giving him more fodder to tease her about.

He did not laugh, however. Bless him for that. "Do you not think you can find a husband here?" he asked, adjusting the brim of his hat.

She shook her head. "Not unless I accept Mr. Dobson."

The look of disgust he sent her way nearly made her laugh.

"Listen, Gracie, I won't tell you all the reasons I think you're wrong about this husband business, because I do not think we are good enough friends yet for you to believe me. But I will say that I hope you find the happiness you're searching for. You deserve it."

His words were always teasing and insincere, but there was not even the smallest hint of sarcasm. She turned her head forward, thinking over his words and noticing the newly falling snow for the first time. The flakes were small, almost imperceptible, but only inches from her nose. How could she not notice something right in front of her?

Like the fact that she and Richard could be friends.

She had always been very aware of him, but somehow after their conversation her senses were heightened. The shift of his arm, the clenching of his jaw, and the way he searched his surroundings and took in every detail. But it was his thoughts she wanted to know better. What else had he endured? Would he keep confiding in her? This was new territory. It should have scared her, but oddly, it did not.

Upon returning to the house and descending the carriage, Richard took her gloved hand in his.

She started to pull back, but he held firm. "Your family is watching." He bent over her hand, and at the last minute, flipped it over, exposing her wrist. His lips pressed against her bare skin, sending a dizzying tingle up her arm. He slowly lifted his head until his gaze reached hers.

"Until next time, Gracie."

She could not bring herself to respond, so utterly stunned by his unexpected kiss. He seemed to guess her thoughts and gave an unrepentant grin. After his carriage pulled away, her eyes flicked to the windows to spot her family.

Not a soul was in sight.

Chapter 11

DESPITE ALL HIS PROMISES to himself that he would do anything to save Belside, Richard had refrained from seeing Grace or Ruth at all the day before. He knew the risk he took wasting precious time, but the right choice was not always the practical one. Instead of games of courtship, he made a special effort to write to his mother and spend time with Bridget. Surprisingly, his sister hadn't abandoned him to be with her dearest friend. She *had* wanted to be with him.

Grace was right. He'd neglected his sister in her time of need. Last night they'd stayed up late reading Father's journal in the library together. Afterward, they'd talked about how they'd felt when they'd heard the news of Father's death and relived those first few weeks. Speaking about feelings and thoughts that Richard had attempted to bury had been cathartic. His previous conversation with Grace had opened a channel he had dammed up, and the pent-up emotion poured through more freely now.

Grace had seen what he could not. Bridget hadn't just needed him; he had needed his sister. When he visited Callis Hall today, he intended to pull Grace aside and thank her. No one else could have been so frank, so honest. She had not only helped his relationship with Bridget, but Ruth was now meeting his eye and speaking to him. It was certainly not enough to secure an engagement, but Grace had known the way to Ruth's heart. He was eager to renew his efforts in courting

Grace and watching Ruth soften, but he would no longer ignore his sister in the process.

Over breakfast, he extended his invitation to Bridget. "Would you care to accompany me to Callis Hall today? I had hoped to meet with Mr. Steele—"

"You mean you'd hoped to meet with Grace," Bridget said, pointing her fork at him. "You do not have to play coy with me. And if it is courtship you want, you might want to think beyond simple visits to the house while Mrs. Steele hovers about."

What was he to say to this? "Since you are so well-versed in these matters, what would you suggest?"

Bridget set down her fork and exchanged it for her half-eaten roll smothered in plum jam. "Well, since you are being so amiable as of late, why not accomplish two tasks at once? I have long desired for you to teach me to fence, and I believe it the perfect sort of activity to invite the Steeles over to join us for."

"Tobias might enjoy sparring, but it is not a ladylike sport. Mr. and Mrs. Steele would never let their daughters near us again."

"Women have fenced before," Bridget complained. "Do you not recall the stories about Catherine Douglass, Duchess of Queensbury?"

"I recall that she was an eccentric woman who many spoke ill of. I do not want that for you or the Misses Steeles."

Bridget finished off her roll and wiped a bit of jam from her finger with her napkin. "Will I never convince you?"

He shook his head. "So will you join me at Callis Hall or not?"

"How about a fencing example then between you and Tobias? Surely, a lady can watch the sport in her own home."

Richard sat back in his chair and folded his arms across his chest. Bridget rarely asked anything from him. Surely a little demonstration wouldn't hurt. "Can you keep this a secret from Mother?"

Bridget crossed her heart and put her hands together to beg.

"Enough. I will send a missive over to the Steeles, but do not be surprised if only Tobias comes."

In the end, it was he who was surprised. Tobias arrived an hour later accompanied by his sisters.

"I am pleased you could come," he said to them.

Grace dipped a curtsy. "Thank you for inviting us." Her cheeks bloomed a subtle shade of pink when her eyes met his, and his stomach clenched at the reaction. Was she remembering the kiss he had left on her wrist? Because he certainly was. Her impossibly soft skin had smelled like spring flowers. A scent he would gladly breathe in again and again. He had not anticipated his impulsive move that day, nor his reaction to it. Nor could he explain why he couldn't chase away thoughts of her as easily as before.

"We are eager to watch the match," Ruth said, distracting his attention.

"Uh, this way to the drawing room. The footmen have moved the furniture back against the wall for the entertainment."

They walked in companionable silence into the room

"It is not every day we have permission to watch a men's sport," Grace said, finding a seat on a sofa.

"Indeed, we *never* have permission," Ruth said, meeting his gaze—a subtle point in his favor. "I have only read about fencing matches in books."

"Aw, but books have high stakes, where this is going to be a short lesson and simple sparring."

Bridget carried in two foils, handing him his blade first. "It's going to be a thrilling afternoon, Richard. Don't downplay it." She went to Tobias next. "Don't hold back," she told him. "My brother can handle it."

"Obviously, I won't win," Tobias answered with a nervous laugh. He set his mask over his head. "Nonetheless, I do expect you ladies to cheer for me."

All three women broke out in a succession of exaggerated cheers, making them all laugh.

Richard put on his own mask. Mother had made him purchase a set of masks during his time at university. She had never been fond of the sport, and while most men preferred to play with their heads back, she had demanded he wear a mask, and Father had enforced it. Now that he was sparring with a much younger opponent, he could see the usefulness of the purchase.

He and Tobias slipped into on guard position. "Hits are only valid on the right breast. Are you ready?"

Tobias gave a quick nod. "I think so." He lunged forward, and Richard easily parried the attack.

"Don't put all your weight on your back leg."

"I thought that was customary," Tobias said.

"It is, but if you can balance more, you will have the advantage in speed. Try again." Out of the corner of his eye, he noticed Grace's riveting gaze on him. Had his instructions to Tobias made him sound conceited? That had not been his point, but he did not like that Grace might construe his words as such. He had not cared before, but after their last talk in the carriage, he was questioning himself and wishing to be better than before.

A moment later, Tobias parried, followed by a timely riposte. "Much better," he said. "Again."

They sparred for a solid forty-five minutes, and finally, Tobias, using a feint-disengage attack maneuver, managed to thrust the end of his foil into Richard's chest. All three women clapped excessively.

Richard joined in the clapping. "Very good! You are a quick learner."

"Thank you." Tobias pulled off his hat, revealing a mop of sweaty hair. "I might need a moment to breathe before we go at it again."

"Have some refreshment." Richard waved him toward the women. Bridget had arranged for queen cakes and tea. He'd half expected to see more shortbread and melted chocolate, but perhaps Richard would have to perform better to earn their favorite treat. He removed his gloves and hat, wiping his face with a handkerchief.

"I am impressed with your talent."

Richard turned to find Grace holding a cup of tea for him to take. He accepted it. "Thank you."

"I have heard many times of your love for the sport, but I did not equate that to the hours of work and practice that came with it. Your dedication is admirable."

A small smile played on his lips. She wasn't forcing out a compliment for anyone to hear this time. It was honest and completely satisfying. "When something is important to you, the sacrifice of time and energy is nothing."

She sipped on her own cup of tea. "I have seen proof of that recently in other areas of your life, but none of those passions included teaching my brother with such utter patience and encouragement."

This he could not take credit for. "Bridget wanted a demonstration. I . . . was trying to do something for her." He fingered the warm porcelain in his hand. "It's because of what you said the other day."

"You listened?" She shook her head in disbelief.

"I did. Friends listen to friends, do they not?"

The awe in her eyes turned to what he hoped was a shade of admiration. He did not need her approval, but for some reason, having it seemed very important to him.

Grace led him over to speak to Ruth, who had a number of questions about the different fencing blades. He happily explained them to her, but his attention was torn. He kept noticing little things he shouldn't. Where Grace was standing. The sound of her laugh. And the lilt of her voice. Each played in the back of his mind long after the Steeles returned home.

Instead of puzzling over why, or trying to chase the curious thoughts away, he let himself contemplate all things Grace. She hadn't shied away when he had needed her, and that meant a great deal to him.

So, he would allow himself to think of her.

Just for one night.

Chapter 12

THE STEELE FAMILY HOSTED a card party every December before the holidays came and families traveled or made family plans. Tomorrow was the day, and Grace was in charge of overseeing the maids' cleaning of the main rooms the guests would frequent. It was a very pointed task, since Grace was not always the most tidy. She liked organization, but she merely prioritized more exciting tasks to the tedious, boring ones.

When Richard arrived for an unexpected visit, carrying a mysterious crate, she was suddenly self-conscious. She wore an old white dimity gown and apron, and her hair was coming out of its coiffure from her attempt to pull a marble out from under the sofa. Brushing aside her embarrassment, she forced her shoulders to straighten. It was only Richard Graham, and there was no need to impress him.

"Why on earth are you carrying that dusty old crate?" Grace asked with a laugh.

"You mean a box of treasures?"

"Treasures?" Now he had her complete attention.

"You aren't the only one who has been cleaning today. Bridget and I went back into the attic this morning after breakfast for a little fun. She helped me pack up a few items your family might enjoy."

She hurried over to him, eager to see what he'd brought. Unfortunately, he was too tall for her to see anything. "Set it down in the corridor. We just beat out the rugs in here."

"So, you won then?" he asked from over the top of the crate on his way back through the drawing room door.

"Won what?"

"You said you beat the rugs."

She snorted. She was a fan of puns and riddles, as he well knew, but this one was very bad. "I am excessively good at winning against rugs. Do you even have to ask? You can set the crate on the side table." She hurried to move the vase back.

He stepped back from the crate and brushed at the line of dust on his waistcoat and the lapels of his jacket. It was no use. The dust wasn't budging.

"You should have thought to wear an apron," she said, now quite proud of her attire. She couldn't imagine Richard, in his dapper clothes, donning such a lowly clothing item.

"Not all of us can look as good in an apron as you do."

Aw, the teasing Richard was back. She picked up the bottom of her apron to relieve him. "Here. Let me help."

She brushed the coarse white fabric against his dark-green jacket. It did help a little.

He picked up the other corner of her apron and started brushing off his other side.

She glanced up at him the same time he met her gaze, and her hand froze. They were standing very close together. And was there. . . heat . . . emanating from his body?

He gave an uneasy chuckle. "I daresay this looks a little awkward."

"Agreed." He dropped her apron the same time she did.

She took a quick step backward, her hands fiddling with her apron strings until they were untied. Removing it, she handed it to him so he could clean his jacket himself.

"Thank you."

She nodded and turned to his crate. It was at a height now that she could see what was inside. Laughing at what she saw, she shook her head. "I don't understand."

He lifted up the white glove on top and handed it to her. "What is not to understand? This is a treasure, just as I said."

"It's so heavy."

"It's one of my old fencing gloves. They are too tight for my hands now, so I thought to make a present out of them for Tobias."

"For me?"

That boy had ears like a hawk. He skipped down the stairs and rounded the corner to where she and Richard stood. It was a good thing he hadn't come a minute or two earlier and caught her and Richard in an awkward position. Tobias took the glove from her hand and grinned. "It's hardly worn."

"I grew three inches the year my father gave those to me. I might have worn them twice. They're yours if you want them."

Mrs. Steele and Ruth came down the corridor from the library. "I thought I heard your voice, Mr. Graham," Mrs. Steele said. "It is so nice seeing you so often. I hope you are coming to our card party tomorrow."

"Of course. Bridget would not let me miss it. She would have accompanied me today, but she is thoroughly diverted playing dress-up with my grandmother's old gowns we discovered in the attic."

Grace put her hand to her mouth to keep from laughing. What would Bridget think when she discovered there were no buttons on them?

Richard pointed to the crate. "We scrounged up a few items to see if they would be of any interest to your family," he explained. He slid out some old sheet music, yellow with age. "This is an original composition by my great-uncle. I thought Ruth might like to see if it was any good."

"Would I ever?" She accepted the pages with a careful touch.

He dug out the next item: a small box. "We thought this was a box of jewelry, but it was beaded fishing lures. Bridget was devastated. I have plenty of lures, so I thought Mr. Steele might like these to use on our pond this summer."

Papa would be overjoyed. He loved to fish but always felt like he was overstepping if he asked to fish at Belside more than once or twice a summer.

"I will accept them for him," Mama said. "Did you rescue a prize for me too?"

"Mama!" Grace said with a laugh.

"I did, indeed." Richard held up a small framed likeness of Callis Hall. "I think my grandmother painted it, but I can barely read the signature. Anyway, it ought to belong here with your family."

"How lovely," Mama cooed. "It does look like your grandmother's work. I only knew her for a short time, but she was a talented woman."

Grace realized she was the last one to receive a gift, but she would not be so presumptuous as Mama. He didn't need to bring her a gift. In fact, after the way she had treated him all these years, he had no reason to.

"Is that it?" Tobias asked, as if reading her mind.

Richard shot a glance at her and smiled. "One left." He dipped his hand in the dusty crate for the last time and pulled out a book.

Whether it was boring or not, she would make herself read it. It was the thought that counted. She extended her hand and accepted it. "Thank you, Mr. Graham. This is most thoughtful."

She opened it to a random page and discovered it blank. It was a journal, not a book.

"I've seen you write in your journal before, and thought you might like it."

She stroked the smooth leather cover. "I filled the last page in my journal weeks ago and have been wanting a new one."

"Filled up with silly riddles, perfume recipes, and a million ways to get out of trouble, no doubt," Ruth teased.

She hadn't been wrong. This was the exact gift she needed. Practical, useful, and perfect for her. Warmth settled around her, and she looked up to meet Richard's gaze.

He leaned against the crate, watching her reaction.

"It is most thoughtful," she assured him. "A true treasure." She added the last bit with an exaggerated emphasis to make him smile. It worked.

"In that case, the deliveries have been made, and I must return to our attic scavenging. I will see you all tomorrow evening." After a bow, he turned around to leave. No one said anything about the dust line on the back of his jacket, but they shared a few snickers behind their hands until the door closed after him.

That night, Grace opened her new journal to write in it only to discover someone had already written a riddle. Intrigued, she read:

A boy you loathe, handsome though he be,
With charms that grow, a grudging kindness you see.
Through chance and time, disdain shall bend,
For in his heart, you'll find a friend.
Who am I?

She grinned and ran her finger over the line about friendship. Richard had surprised her. He was making a real effort to change. Perhaps she did not despise him so very much. Even if he did call himself handsome in his riddle. Her scoff was part laugh. That was so perfectly like him.

And more than a little bit true.

Chapter 13

WHEN THE CARRIAGE ARRIVED at Callis Hall for the card party, Richard assisted Bridget out into the cold night, sheltering her tall, willowy form the best he could while they hurried up the steps. The wind was especially brisk tonight, and it chased them all the way inside.

Once they had shed their outer clothing, they followed Mr. Reed into the drawing room, which hummed with the chatter of guests. Something in the air smelled of the holidays almost upon them—perhaps it was the wood burning in the grate, or the smell of punch, or a mere idea in his head, but it was there all the same. Several tables had been set up about the room, but no one was sitting quite yet. They were clustered in small groups about the room, visiting.

"It's a larger group than I anticipated." A thrill of excitement filled Bridget's voice. With Mother gone, Richard did not think it inappropriate for her to attend a party. They couldn't keep her at home forever.

"Enjoy every minute," Richard instructed. "That's an order."

Bridget laughed at his playful tone. "Look, there is Ruth. She must be expiring with the sheer numbers. Perhaps I should go and set her at ease."

Richard had always thought his sister kind, but her age was known to be a selfish one. He was notably impressed with her thoughtfulness.

He intended to follow Bridget, but in a moment of weakness, his eyes sought out Grace.

He found her by the fireplace, her gown an elegant but simple pink muslin. She was speaking to . . . to Mr. Craig. He had not realized the Steeles were acquainted with Craig. He wasn't from Wetherfield, and Richard only knew him from his time at Oxford, as they were in the same graduating class together. Craig was a decent sort of fellow—handsome and obnoxiously driven. He took one step toward him, with the intention to greet him, when Grace laughed.

Richard's jaw reflexively flinched. He continued his path toward them, stopping to take a quick bow to Mrs. Steele in passing before reaching the pair by the fireplace.

"I had no idea Wetherfield had such fine company," Mr. Craig said to Grace, his smile lined with pleasure.

"Until you showed up," Richard inserted, stepping beside Grace.

"Graham!" Craig grinned. "What the devil are you doing here?"

Richard's own smile was not so wide, but he didn't quite understand why. Shouldn't he be happy to see an old school chum? "My estate neighbors Callis Hall."

"So, I have you to blame for not telling me about the hidden gems here." Craig's gaze shifted back to Grace's.

Was she blushing? Why did she blush so easily for Craig when it took Richard so much effort? "Yes, you can blame me. We do not give up our treasures easily." He set his hand on the small of Grace's back. Besides the kiss to her hand, he hadn't touched her like this since their ice-skating, and it wasn't as acceptable here as it was there. But he couldn't bring himself to remove it. Instead, he shifted ever closer to her until she was firmly by his side.

Craig's brow rose.

Well, they were courting, weren't they? Shouldn't everyone know it?

Grace's voice came out strained. "I see my mother is waving me over. Excuse me."

Richard's hand instantly fell, and both he and Craig instinctively followed her line of vision to see Mrs. Steele with Mrs. Peterson and a young woman he did not recognize. She was pretty in a showy sort of way, her dress overtrimmed next to Grace's, and a large bow pinned to her hair. Was this Mrs. Peterson's niece? He heard that she might visit, and it was clear Mrs. Steele wanted Grace to befriend the woman.

Craig nudged him with his elbow. "My sister is a diamond of the first water. Don't you agree?"

"Your sister?"

"Yes, we decided to come visit our aunt and uncle for the holidays. How fortunate to find we are among friends as well."

Richard wasn't feeling overly friendly, but he did possess some manners. "I welcome you both then."

"Come, let me introduce you."

Once they met the others, Richard put himself beside Grace again. He felt like he was standing guard, protecting Grace from the Craigs as the brother and sister answered general questions about their lives. Mr. Craig was not a pariah, but Richard didn't want him getting any ideas of romance. Grace might not be for him, but he was positive Craig was not her equal. The man was a flirt of the highest order and in no hurry to settle down. Richard doubted that anything had changed in the eighteen months since they had seen each other last.

After a few minutes of visiting, they were ushered to a table to begin a game. He had hoped to end up at a table with Bridget and Ruth, but instead sat down with the Craigs and Grace. Bridget and Ruth took a table next to theirs. Richard caught Ruth's eye and sent her a friendly smile. It was reciprocated, followed by a pointed look at her sister Grace, seated next to him, and a slight nod.

What was that supposed to mean? Was she encouraging him to court Grace? Or beat her at whist? He would have to think about it more later.

He glanced at Grace, who was oblivious of the small exchange. She was too busy whispering with Bridget, whose chair was back-to-back with her own. The two of them complimented each other's gowns and hair before turning around to begin their prospective games. In the meantime, Miss Craig sat opposite him and would be his partner in whist. Lucky him.

"I have no doubt that you are an excellent card player, Mr. Graham," Miss Craig said, commanding his attention. Her chin dipped toward one shoulder and her lashes fluttered in a practiced pose.

"I am fair," he admitted, feigning focus on his fingernail.

Miss Craig picked up her fan. "No need to be modest."

"Mr. Graham is never modest," Grace quipped. "He is objectively fair at whist when paired with a partner of equal skill."

Richard almost snorted, but a quick swipe of his nose prevented any rude sounds from omitting.

Craig chuckled. "And what of you, Miss Steele? Are you a regular card shark?" There was plenty of flirtation in Craig's voice, and Richard's hand nearly crumpled his cards. She was not his next conquest. The mere thought nearly made him growl.

Grace shook her head. "Young ladies are never card sharks, Mr. Craig, but I will try not to disappoint you with my abilities."

Now who was being modest? At least she seemed to be intelligent enough not to melt into a puddle over Craig's remarks. Richard leaned back in his chair, trying to shake off his attack pose.

The first round was played with painful slowness. The Craigs preferred to banter with their partners and cared little about strategy. Each time Grace laughed at something Craig said, Richard's temper flared and his smile barely hid his gritted teeth. But why? Why was jealousy pillaging his reason and leaving it to hang from the rafters? Nothing had felt the same between them since their frank conversation on their carriage ride and his impulsive decision to kiss her wrist. But she was not his intended, and letting Craig flirt with her could be good for her future.

Grace won the first trick, and a few minutes later, the second.

"How did I manage to secure the best partner?" Craig asked, giving a subtle wink. Richard caught it and his careful social face disappeared behind furrowed brows. How dare he take such liberties. They had met not a half hour ago.

Miss Craig gave her brother a pouting face. "Not the best. No one can compare to Mr. Graham." Her head turned toward him and produced another round of eyelash flutters.

Grace set a card down. "Indeed, when Mr. Graham concentrates on his hand, he can play exceptionally well."

The dig made him swing his eyes to hers. So he had played badly this round. How was he supposed to concentrate with this ridiculous conversation happening before him?

She narrowed her eyes so quickly he almost missed it.

Why was *she* mad? She was supposed to be courting *him*, not falling for a perfect stranger. His long knee swung to the side to nudge her leg.

Her leg nudged him back, and not in a gentle, romantic way either. She *was* mad.

As subtly as he could, he motioned his head toward the floor.

Her brow quirked in confusion, but she quickly turned away so no one would see.

A few moments passed before he caught her eye again. This time with his hand between them, he motioned to the floor.

Her look of exasperation nearly stole all his ire and made him laugh, but he resisted. They needed to talk. He motioned again.

Grace let her hand of cards flutter to the floor. "Dear me."

"Let me help," Richard said. They both lowered to the ground and shifted under the tablecloth to reach the fallen cards.

"What is wrong with you?" Grace hissed. "You're positively sullen and glaring at everyone."

He leaned close so they wouldn't be overheard. "What is wrong with me? What about you?"

She shook her pretty head and whispered, "I've done nothing wrong."

His nose nearly touched hers, and he was drawn to her like water in a desert. "Besides flirting with strangers." He didn't know what he was doing, but whatever it was, he seemed to have lost all self-control.

"Speak for yourself!" Her eyes, a bright green, seemed to dare him to say otherwise, but it was a breathlessness in her voice that snagged on something in his chest.

"I'm trying to be your friend and . . ."

Why wasn't she pulling away? Richard lost all the fight in his tone and tried to blink away the sudden tumult of feeling. He made the mistake of dropping his gaze to her mouth—rose pink, the bottom lip slightly fuller than the top. His heart pounded. A thread of desire stitched the air between them, cinching them ever closer.

He was going to kiss her.

"Did you lose a card?" Craig asked, pulling up the tablecloth.

Richard jerked back, knocking his head on the underside of the table. Grace's smaller form slipped out from under the table with far more finesse.

"Not at all," Grace said, her voice shaky but self-assured. "Mr. Graham was kneeling on one, but they've all been rescued." He caught a subtle tremble in her hand, but by the time she climbed back to her seat, she appeared completely unruffled and intent on avoiding his gaze.

The rest of the game passed with a blur. His anger no longer simmered. It had been replaced with a glimmer of fear.

He had nearly kissed her.

Little Gracie May . . . his sister's best friend . . . his greatest antagonist.

And the worst part?

He was thoroughly sorry he hadn't.

Chapter 14

It took Grace three days to recover from the card party before finally deciding she was strong enough to visit Bridget without conjuring up images of her brother under the card table. She might never forget how his light-brown eyes had burned gold when he'd glanced at her mouth, or how his warm breath had tickled her lips. An abundance of feelings had tumbled through her: disappointment, curiosity, fascination. None of them made sense. The primary emotion should be relief and none else. She shook her head to clear it as a footman let her inside Belside manor.

"Miss Graham is in the library, miss."

"Thank you, Nevell." She handed him her cloak and made her way to the library.

She glanced toward the closed study door, wondering if Richard was sequestered inside or out with his friends. She hoped it was the latter. She had expressly come in the early afternoon, knowing he was an active personality who usually was out and about on business or errands at this time of day. She did not make it a habit of noticing his schedule, but since she did not care to see him today, she had put more thought into it than usual.

A creak sounded behind her and she jumped.

Good heavens. It was the maid.

She clung to her throat. Was she afraid of Richard now? This sort of behavior was ridiculous. True, she had barely handled seeing him the day after the card party for his short visit. He had said a few words to her, and she had caught a few strange looks as well, but he had spent the majority of the time asking Ruth about her music.

All this time, Grace had not known him to be so enraptured on the subject. A perfect reminder that he cared for her sister and not her. If she had any reason to believe his feelings had shifted to her, that visit had cleared up any misunderstanding.

Even so, when Richard had left that day, she had felt both relieved and disappointed. He stopped by again yesterday with Bridget but, thank the stars, she had been in town with Mother at the mercantile. She had been wise to beg her mother to buy her a new pair of gloves. The time apart had been just what her senses needed to recover from a dreadful Richard Graham hangover. The man was as toxic as any strong drink, and she was determined to stay sober. Their secret arrangement had merely confused her. In less than a month's time, he would be engaged to her sister, and she would move away to find a suitor of her own.

She pulled the walnut door open and found Bridget on the ladder, tugging a book off a high shelf. Her head turned and her gaze met Grace's. "Finally, you have come. It has been an age!"

"Three days," Grace corrected.

Bridget climbed down, tucking her book under her arm. "As I said, an age. I know you were in town yesterday, but you must have a better excuse for not visiting me."

She had a most valid excuse, but one she intended to keep to herself. "We cannot be together every day," she said. "What will happen when I move to my aunt's?"

Bridget tucked her arm in Grace's. "I don't worry about that anymore because it is not going to happen."

Grace met her gaze square in the eyes. "I haven't convinced my parents yet, but I am determined."

Bridget led her to a floral sofa in tans and pinks, its high back a similar walnut color as the door and shelves lining the walls. "You cannot lie to me. I have known you much too long."

"Why would I lie?"

Bridget spread her arm across the back of the sofa, in the very pose her brother often adopted, and Grace had to look away. "See, that look! You do not want to leave, do you?"

Grace sighed. "I have to leave. I want to get married, and I haven't any suitors here." She purposefully did not mention how Mr. Craig had called on her the day before yesterday. She was not yet sure of his interest. He seemed the type to prefer conquests to marriage. And she wasn't desperate enough to consider Mr. Dobson after working so hard to be rid of his attentions.

"How could you say that? My poor brother is exhausting himself chasing after you. I wish you would forgive him and give him a chance."

"He is hardly chasing me. Besides, he ignored you and your mother in your time of need." Even as she said it, her ire toward him on that subject had waned considerably.

"We talked about it, you know." Bridget brought her arms down and set them in her lap. "He told me what you said and apologized. Then he spent the days leading up to the card party doing whatever I wanted him to do. It was the most fun I've had in a long time."

"The most fun? I thought we had fun regularly." Grace gave a playful shake of her head.

"You know what I mean. I've missed him."

Grace nodded, grateful that they had reconciled.

Bridget nudged her. "So, can you forgive him too? He loves you."

Grace choked on her next breath and coughed into her sleeve. "Love . . . love is a strong word, Bridget. You cannot throw it about so casually."

Bridget grinned. "I am in perfect earnest. I've been watching you two for weeks. Sparks have always flown between you when you sparred words, but I do believe they have finally ignited."

"Good heavens. Sparks? Honestly, Bridget. You have read too many romances of late." They had made progress in their friendship, but that hardly was the makings of a romance.

"I know my brother better than anyone, Grace. He is smitten!"

She reviewed his compliment about looking well in an apron the day he had visited with his treasures. What if he hadn't been teasing? And then she remembered the look when their eyes had met and their near position.

She needed a fan. The fire behind the grate seemed suffocatingly warm. "It is an act, Bridget," she hurried to say. "I wanted to tell you, but I didn't know how."

Bridget's brown eyes lowered. "I don't believe it."

"It's true. He is interested in Ruth. He's pretending to court me to get to my sister. I'm sorry I did not say anything sooner, but I was trying to protect his feelings."

She waited for Bridget's anger to come, but instead a laugh poured out of her mouth. "And you believed him? I thought you were too intelligent to fall for such a silly falsehood. You cannot pretend what I see when Richard looks at you. Nor, might I add, how you look in return."

"Is it hot in here to you?" Her face felt flushed. "I'm starting to feel ill. Should I open up a window?"

"It's the perfect temperature," Bridget said. "But I can understand if I am pushing too much. If it will make you happy, I will go along with your idea that Richard is interested in Ruth. And we shall see who is right in the end."

Grace's sigh reached her toes. "Thank you, Bridget. I do not want you to get attached to the idea that your brother and I . . . that we . . ."

"That we . . . what?" Richard asked from the doorway.

She glanced up and met his amused smirk. It set her heart pattering in her chest like a little cupid dancing there. "That we have plans to kill each other," she said quickly.

He gave an exaggerated frown, leaning into the doorframe like a brooding fictional hero posing for a portrait that women would worship for centuries to come. "I thought we were friends, Gracie May. I could never willingly hurt you, and I know you care too much to wound me."

His emphasis on her caring rattled her. Did he know? Had he sensed her hidden weakness?

She scowled as she had done for years every time he had sent her his disarming smile. "Is it even possible to hurt such an inflated ego?"

He pretended to think the question over, even stroking his chin as he did. "No, I don't believe it is."

"Then, I suppose since I am ill-equipped with knowledge or skills to fight, and my words do little to affect you, you are safe . . . for now."

"Ah, you intrigue me. It is almost as if you mentioned me and your future in the same sentence. How endearing that you imagine remaining in my company when you clearly pretend otherwise."

She snorted.

Bridget laughed into a pillow. "You two are terrible. What am I supposed to do with you both?" She clapped her hands. "I know. I've had a hankering to make a craft. It'll be ever so much fun, and there will be no time for petty arguments."

Grace opened her mouth to object, but Richard beat her to it.

"As much as I adore crafts," Richard said, heavy with sarcasm, "I really have more pressing business. I do hope you have a lovely time." He started to retreat when Bridget called after him.

"You can't say no, Richard. You owe me more of your time."

His shoulders fell and he turned back around. "Now?"

"Yes, now."

"But a craft, really?"

"Really."

Grace groaned and not quietly either. There was no reason to put on airs here. She had hoped for a quiet visit with Bridget and absolutely no time in Richard's company. "I suppose I can stay a few minutes longer, but I really ought to return to my parents . . . to . . . help choose . . . the soup."

"The soup?" Bridget looked disbelieving.

"For dinner."

"Not fair," Richard said, coming into the room. "My excuse was legitimate, and I'm not allowed out of this craft business. You're clearly lying, so you should have to stay even longer than I do."

Her ability to think of clever plans was waning. Richard's presence was clouding her thoughts. Relenting, she leaned back into her seat. "I just remembered. My mother always chooses the soup. What craft are we doing, and how can I help?"

"I love your attitude," Richard said.

"Yes, thank you, Grace. I expect the same commitment from you, brother."

Richard gave a grave nod. "I can do anything Grace can do."

"Good," Bridget said. "Because we are making mistletoe kissing boughs."

Grace's gaze flashed to Richard's. He met it with a look of incredulousness that surely matched her own. What on earth had they just agreed to?

"It will likely take a few days." Bridget stood and started ticking items off her fingers. "We must find baskets and ribbons, cut pine and holly branches, and of course, find ourselves some mistletoe."

"How many are we making?" Richard hedged.

Bridget squinted, as if thinking carefully. "I daresay we'll need at least a dozen."

"A dozen?" It was Richard's turn to choke and cough. "What would we do with a dozen kissing boughs?"

Thankfully, he didn't meet Grace's eye this time. She would have melted into the cushions beneath her.

Bridget laughed. "They aren't for us. We'll keep one and gift the others. If I remember correctly from last year, they should stay fresh for two whole weeks. We can deliver them on Christmas Eve when everyone begins to decorate."

"Just what we need," Richard said with a small huff. "For the whole town to turn into a kissing fest."

"What a romantic notion." Bridget's sigh was full of wistfulness. "I thought you were a lost cause, Richard, but you're redeeming yourself quite well."

She knew Bridget was jesting, and not only that, she was scheming too. How could Grace turn this to work in her favor? She couldn't continue to spend so much time with Richard and keep herself sane. Besides, she had agreed to support his goals too. She cleared her throat. "It sounds like a great deal of work." Grace folded her hands primly in her lap, hopefully looking extremely innocent.

"Oh, yes," Bridget insisted. "It will take long hours together."

"My thoughts exactly," Grace said. "I vote we include Ruth to help us."

"Ruth?" Bridget scowled. She leaned toward Grace and hissed, "What are you trying to do?"

She kept her face passive. "Nothing. We established this is a large project, and Ruth has an artistic eye."

"What a brilliant idea," Richard said, smiling gratefully at her. "Ruth will make an excellent addition."

Grace relaxed as she had not done since Richard entered the room. Nothing had been normal between them since the beginning of December, but with a little ingenuity, their plans could still work.

Chapter 15

RICHARD'S MOUTH FORMED A grim line as he studied the papers in his hand, the numbers burning holes behind his eyes.

"They won't change no matter how long you stare at them."

Richard looked up at Mr. Bowers, his new solicitor. He had thin brown hair, sharp but compassionate eyes, and an unpretentious but tidy suit of clothes. Richard had hired him after Father's death. Father's solicitor was old enough to be a gnarled tree in a different century, and his memory issues had caused a number of drastic problems for the estate. Mr. Bowers had done his best with what they had left, but their latest investment had not produced the desired results fast enough.

"I know," Richard said, dropping the papers onto his desk. Mentally, he listed a few improvements the estate needed. A tenant home required a new roof come spring, much of their farming equipment was outdated, and the manor house was in constant need of upkeep. He rubbed his eyes with his thumb and forefinger, whispering a silent plea to the heavens for help.

"You'll have to let the house or sell," Mr. Bowers said.

"Closing off the west wing doesn't seem to have helped anything?" He knew the answer, but he had to ask anyway. What if they closed off everything but two bedchambers and the drawing room?

"It cut back on a few costs, but they were pennies compared to what you need."

Richard felt a knot of anxiety growing in his chest. "We could reduce the staff to a skeletal crew." He had been against this before, wanting to keep his mother and sister in comfort, but he was willing to do anything before he'd sell or rent it out.

"It might buy you more time."

Time. He was just as short in it as he was in funds. He did not have to look at the calendar to know that he had only two weeks until his deadline with his aunt. Fourteen measly days to convince Ruth to marry him. He'd already missed the opportunity to post the banns and have them read the three weeks before the wedding. While he had a special license, it did not guarantee a bride to go with it.

Everything was getting out of hand. He'd been hopeful before, but it felt ill-placed now. It was growing harder to pretend cheerfulness around Bridget and to not succumb to the worry building inside him.

Richard scratched at his jaw, thinking over his options. "I will keep the staff on over the holidays. Let's meet again directly after, and I will have a decision for you."

"Very well, Mr. Graham." Mr. Bowers reached for his satchel. "I hope you will consider letting it go. I know that this house and land are filled with your family's history, but a few years in a small cottage could be just the solution to grow your investments and pay down debt."

"A few years?"

"Ten . . . twelve at most."

Richard hadn't the energy to cry, but he planned to use these blasted papers to wipe up his tears when he did. They represented all he was about to lose.

"I have a lot to think about. Thank you for your time, Mr. Bowers."

"Good day, sir."

Richard saw him out and stared at the closed door for some time, lost in his thoughts. A trill of laughter sounded from somewhere in the house, and it pulled him from his woolgathering.

Grace was here.

The thought lightened his mood. It shouldn't have, but more and more this past month, she had been the only person capable of distracting him from the pressure of his situation.

She seemed convinced that he could win Ruth over, and her surety had been an anchor to his drifting will power. The day before yesterday, they had collected Ruth and gone to town to purchase all sorts of festive ribbons. He had been tight with Bridget's pin money, but she had asked for so little this last year that he had indulged her. It had been a relief to see the store had advertised a sale in their window, cutting down the overall expenditure.

When had he ever worried about the cost of ribbons?

He hadn't even realized he'd been walking until he drew close to the drawing room door. He wanted to see Grace. Needed to see her.

His hand hovered on the handle. Was he falling in love with her? He yanked away from the offending brass. Admittedly, he'd been more attracted to her than ever, and she was never far from his thoughts . . . but that was because of the added time they were in each other's company.

He couldn't love Grace.

It would ruin everything.

The knot in his chest grew to the size of an orange, pressing on his lungs and making his breathing shallow. He opened the door, and his eyes immediately snagged on Grace's profile. Her sweet little pixie nose and bright intelligent eyes, and the curve of her pink mouth as she lifted her teacup to her lips. Oxygen filled his chest at the mere sight of her.

He ignored what it meant, pushing into the room.

"Richard!" Bridget cried when she noticed him. Her bright smile lifted his thoughts too. She would forgive him if they lost Belside, he knew that now, but she shouldn't have to. "Your timing is impeccable. Ruth thinks she knows of a place we can find mistletoe."

He hadn't even noticed Ruth, sitting just beyond Bridget.

"Oh?"

Ruth nodded, her mannerisms subdued next to her sister's. "There is an apple orchard behind our estate. It belongs to Mr. Callingworth. He lets me walk there when I have a mind to. I noticed some mistletoe growing in the trees on my last walk. We will need a servant to help fetch it."

Ruth's voice was quiet but steady and still so unfamiliar to him after all these years as her neighbor. But she was warming to him, that he could tell.

"A fine idea, Miss Steele," he acknowledged. "Our gardener, Mr. Peters, loves a challenge. I will ask him if he is available. Should I have the carriage readied?" A bit of cold, fresh air sounded like just the thing to snap him from his mood.

"Oh, yes," Bridget said. "We cannot continue on our project without our mistletoe."

He left the room long enough to send a servant to ready the carriage and ask for Mr. Peters's assistance. When he returned, the women stood to gather their cloaks.

"This mistletoe business sounds like more treasure hunting," Grace said to him, coming around the sofa toward him, while Ruth and Bridget continued to discuss their plans. "No one is allowed to stop me if I decide to climb one of these trees to fetch the berries myself."

He smirked. "No one could stop you from doing anything should you have a mind to. Even if we tried."

She made a face. "Certainly not you. If you tell me no, then I will only be more determined."

"And if I say yes?"

"Hmm, good question. Then I will probably still do it."

He shook his head. She was already distracting him, and he was so thankful for it. "Then you want me to agree with you on everything?"

"That would make my life easier."

He wanted to agree with her then and there, forever. All she had to do was ask something of him, and he would be a fool enough to do it. He held the drawing room door open a little wider, allowing her to pass through it. "What about in reverse? Would you make my life easier and agree with me on everything too?"

"Maybe on a few things, since I can be generous, but not everything." He did not know if it was intentional or not, but in that moment, she looked back at Ruth and frowned.

Was she starting to believe that Ruth would never marry him? It wasn't the sort of news he needed at the moment.

When Grace met his gaze again, her frown was gone and she produced a small smile. "What's wrong, Richie? You seem out of sorts."

He hadn't expected her question. "Me?"

"Yes, you."

"I know I can be very disagreeable where you're concerned, but I have been trying harder lately. I did promise to listen too, remember?"

She eyed him, taking his measure in an exaggerated fashion. "You have been marginally better. I've noticed."

He grinned. "Have you?"

"Yes." She dropped her pretense and clasped her hands together in front of her skirt. "You smile more readily."

"I do?"

She nodded. "I believe you've improved in other areas too."

"How so?"

"You seem to care more about what's happening around you."

"I hope so. You know, you've changed too."

"Me?"

He reached up and tapped her cheek. "You blush more."

Her face burned the moment the words left his mouth. "I . . . I do?" She covered her cheeks with her hands.

Without thinking, he set his hands on her wrists and pulled her hands down. "Don't. I like your blush."

He watched her slow swallow. "Why?"

He reluctantly released her. "It's pretty."

He might have to marry her sister one day, but this seemed like something important he needed to say.

She stared at him, disbelieving. "If you're trying to get out of confiding in me, it's working."

He grinned. "If you're trying to cheer me up, it's working."

She laughed. "I don't even know what's bothering you."

He looked over her head at Bridget to assure she was still occupied. "But you noticed, and you genuinely cared to ask about it. In truth, it's nothing new. I had a lovely meeting with my solicitor with more grave news about Belside."

"Oh, Richard. I'm so sorry. What can I do to help? There has to be something."

He reached up and touched her elbow. "You are helping. We've made progress, haven't we?"

She sighed. "Have we?"

"Mr. Dobson is out of the picture and," he lowered his voice, "Ruth actually speaks to me now."

"But your timeline?"

He sighed. He should have proposed by now and posted the bans. "I know."

Bridget and Ruth came up behind them. "What are you two talking about?" Bridget asked. "Grace looks like she is going to cry."

"Who me?" Grace produced a shaky laugh. "I daresay you imagined it. Let's fetch our cloaks and start our treasure hunt."

They proceeded from the room, Grace ushering the women through the door. She looked back at him over her shoulder and whispered. "It will all work out. I know it."

The problem felt too big to fix, but he found himself trusting her once again. He believed Grace capable of anything. And having her on his side this time felt like wind lifting his heavy sails and propelling him toward home.

Chapter 16

GRACE HAD NEVER BEEN mistletoe hunting before. Ruth had led them directly to an apple tree and pointed out the small cluster of plant growth in the otherwise sleeping limb.

"Mistletoe is such a strange plant, is it not?" Richard asked her.

Grace studied the small, creeping plant. "I admit, I have never been mistletoe hunting before. In my ignorance, I thought it grew like a blueberry shrub."

"And here I thought you knew everything," he said.

"I like words and clever turns of phrase, but I am not the bookish sister, remember? The majority of what I have learned in this life is based solely on experience."

The Grahams' gardener sent his son scaling the tree to fetch the mistletoe for them. Not more than twelve, the lad moved like a spider. She watched him as she spoke. "I wish I knew more, read more, studied more. Ruth seems to know a little of everything. I envy her diligence."

"Yes, but Ruth would never have snuck into her neighbor's house to bring her best friend's brother food when he had been sent to his room without dinner."

"You knew about that?" She had forgotten. It had been years ago.

He nodded. "You left the front door open and trailed mud behind you. You were easy enough to follow."

She laughed and the others looked her way. She waited until everyone was once again enthralled by the actions of the boy in the tree. "You covered for us and lied that you had broken the vase when it was our fault." Richard had plenty of redeeming moments, but she had forgotten most of them. Now she wondered how she could have forgotten this particular memory.

"What really happened to that vase?"

"You mean, you did not even know why you lied for us? We had let the new puppies into the house, and we were so worried they'd kill one of them if we told the truth."

"I didn't need a reason other than trying to protect my baby sister and her friend. I believed that you hadn't done it on purpose and feared you'd get a greater punishment than you deserved. Now that I know the truth, I can see why you stole away to the stables after sneaking me dinner."

"You *were* following me!"

He shrugged, tucking his gloved hands beneath his folded arms. "You were an intriguing little thing even then."

Was he implying she was now too?

After they collected their first basketful of mistletoe, they agreed to keep searching the orchard for more plants. She wanted to ask what other memories Richard had about their childhood, but she needed to uphold her end of the bargain, and this was the perfect opportunity to do so.

"Ruth," Grace called to her sister, who was at least a dozen feet ahead of them.

Ruth stopped and turned back to them. "Yes?"

"Mr. Graham did not know that mistletoe was a parasitic plant. Since you've read about them, perhaps you could explain to him what that means."

Richard eyed her. "I thought it was you who was ignorant."

She discreetly pinched his arm. "Play along," she whispered.

When they caught up to Ruth, she quietly began explaining how the mistletoe grew. Grace took the opportunity to step ahead and join Bridget, letting Richard and Ruth have time alone together. Despite her confusing feelings, she wouldn't go back on her word. Helping Richard meant helping Bridget. It was the right thing to do.

A few hours later, they reconvened in the Grahams' drawing room with their baskets of mistletoe, ribbons, and freshly trimmed pine that the servants had gathered for them.

Bridget launched into her leadership role. "Ruth, you sort the mistletoe into bunches. Grace and Richard, you two layer the baskets with pine. I will start cutting strips of ribbon."

A footman had set up a few card tables, and Grace followed Richard to the one Bridget had designated for them. They began quietly working, an air of curious tension sitting between them like a third person.

Grace's eyes settled on Richard's sideburns cut into an L shape at his cheekbone. Trimmed to perfection, they enhanced his already sculpted face. A face she had almost kissed a few days previously under a table much like this one. How could she think about Ruth when thinking at all seemed useless with Richard so near her? With all he had happening in his life, he had dropped everything to agree to making these silly kissing boughs for his sister. He'd been hiding his good heart from her, but now that she knew it was there, she couldn't unsee it.

Richard turned, catching her in her shameless stare. "Admiring something?"

She squirmed, picking up a handful of pine needles and shoving them into the nearest basket. "What do you mean?"

"You were staring."

"Oh, that. I was wondering how you manage to bear all that hubris in that large head of yours."

His lazy smile made her insides dance. "And I was wondering what is so attractive about my big head that you cannot look away."

She scoffed, but still her cheeks burned. "What are you talking about?"

His golden brown eyes sparked a warmth inside her. "You were leaning toward me too."

She straightened, her breathing quickening. Had she really been leaning? There was no need to panic. She could come up with a reasonable explanation. She looked at Ruth carefully sorting the dainty mistletoe on the tea table and Bridget methodically cutting ribbon from the sofa. "You are mistaken. Leaning requires wanting, and I was not . . ." She tried to remember if she had indeed been leaning and couldn't honestly say she hadn't been. What was it about him? She cleared her throat. "A little humility from you would be required to hold my attention." Which was exactly why she had struggled since their carriage ride. He had shown her the real man behind his arrogant facade.

Indeed, he had shown true remorse when she had told him about his neglect toward Bridget, and according to her, he had spent the entire week by his sister's side. She could hardly believe it. He had put his sister's emotional well-being before the future of their estate. He had spent over a year chasing ideas to save Belside, and when put on a deadline to marry Ruth by Twelfth Night for the exact solution, he had willingly stepped away from it.

If he had been attractive at all to Grace before, which was quite the understatement, he was exponentially more so now. Such an amount of attraction seemed impossible to achieve, but drat that man, he had done it.

Any man with eyes could make a fortune if they had bet that she had been leaning toward Richard. She had likely been drooling too. The whole thing exasperated her to no end. Why him? Why not anyone else in the entire world?

"You're much too fun to tease," he said. "But since you have been so dutiful at helping me get to know Ruth, I must try harder to repent of my ways. What is this humility you speak of, and how might I acquire it?"

She elbowed him and he chuckled.

"I'm being serious. You've been telling me for years that I have far too much self-importance. I don't like the man I used to be before Father died. I was too ignorant of significant matters and of the people I truly valued. I want to improve myself. What do you suggest?"

She pointed a small pine branch at him that was no bigger than her hand. "When did you start listening to me?"

"Maybe I've always been listening."

She shook her head. "Remember the time that I warned you that those berries in the back of the house would make you sick? You didn't listen and ate them anyway. You were sick all day. You have always believed that nothing bad could ever happen to you, and that you knew better than everyone else."

He tried to hide a laugh behind his hand, but she saw it clearly.

"I'm glad you can laugh about it now. Despite my criticism, being positive is an admirable trait."

"I'm laughing because I wasn't sick."

Her eyes narrowed. "You weren't?"

"No, I faked it so you and Bridget would play nurse to me. I have to say, those young, skinny arms of yours were stronger than they looked. I cannot believe how long you fanned me. And all those books and drinks you two fetched—such kindness made an impression." He winked at her.

Her stomach flipped. Immediately she remembered how Mr. Craig had winked at her at their card party, but she had had no reaction then. Not like she was experiencing now.

"You're a liar, Richard Graham."

"I have had my share of failings."

This time she dropped her pine and pointed her finger at him. "And what about being repentant?"

He took her hand and crossed his heart with her finger. "I'm a changed man."

She stole back her hand, her skin creeping with heat. His lack of sincerity, of depth, had always bothered her, and she wanted—needed—to reassure herself that he was serious. "How will I know you're sincere?"

He sighed. "Because losing my father and the thought of losing this place . . . it's made me realize what really matters to me. And it's not my own happiness."

The intensity of his gaze and the conviction in his tone were unmistakable. She believed him. In fact, she was starting to think he wasn't the only one changing. She was starting to notice a few things different about herself. And the way she viewed Richard was at the top of her list.

Chapter 17

ALL THE SERVANTS AT Belside were in a fray of activity decorating the house for the holidays. Richard always appreciated their efforts, but he had never joined in the preparations. Today was a first, and strangely, he was looking forward to it. Or had he been looking forward to spending more time with Grace? She had dominated his thoughts from the moment he had awoken.

Richard assisted first Bridget and then Ruth into his carriage, but as soon as Grace accepted his hand, he held her back. He didn't have anything in particular he wanted to say to her, just a minute to see if he had been imagining the shift between them.

Beneath her straw bonnet, a pair of curious sapphire-emerald eyes met his. "Yes?"

He grinned. She was pretty in a bonnet. In a low voice he asked, "Any tips for today, Gracie?"

"Why of course, Richie dear," she whispered. Her lips formed a straight line and her eyes glimmered. "Be impressive."

He chuckled and let her in the carriage. He had expected her to give him something specific to do or say, but Grace was a complex character and never so simple. He should have known. Just as he should have realized that he had imagined nothing. There was something simmering between them. But what to do about it?

Upon sitting next to Bridget, he asked. "Where first?"

"To our dearest friends," Bridget said. "I think we should start with the Petersons."

Richard scratched his cheek that itched as it warmed from the icy breeze outside their carriage. "What about Miss Coleridge? She is on the way there, and we have made more than enough." He didn't know Miss Coleridge well, as she was a few years his senior, but she was one of their closest neighbors.

"The spinster?" Bridget frowned and looked at Grace. "Would she be offended?"

Grace tapped her chin. "It's hard to say. Her temperament is so even-natured that I believe she would be grateful to be thought of."

"Ruth?" Richard asked.

She shrugged. "Why not?"

Richard smiled. "There we have it. Our first stop is Miss Coleridge's."

When they reached Miss Coleridge's house, she beamed over her gift. "How thoughtful! Now I can finally trap a man into marrying me." Her mirth was contagious, and they all laughed and schemed over which man in the neighborhood would be her lucky suitor. Richard had left any party planning to his mother, but he made a note to include Miss Coleridge in their next gathering if they managed to save Belside. She was a delight, and he had a few friends that would appreciate her quick wit and ready smile.

The hours passed quickly as they delivered kissing bough after kissing bough—each a little different in size and style. If the rumors of his attention to the Steele sisters hadn't been confirmed at the card party, they certainly would today. He wasn't afraid for himself, but thoughts of how it would wound Grace's reputation in coming days filled him with worry. He knew she planned to use it as her method of escaping Wetherfield, but it bothered him more than ever.

"That's all of the names on our list," Ruth said, relaxing back into the upholstered carriage seat.

"There are still three left," Grace said, holding up a few smaller ones they had created with remnants. "What should we do with them?"

"We could bring them home with us," Bridget suggested.

Richard balked. "What would we do with kissing boughs in every corner?"

Bridget raised a brow and eyed him, then Grace. "I am sure you could think of something."

He felt his cheeks tinge with a subtle warmth. Him. Blushing? He cleared his throat. "I have a better idea. I have a few tenant families that might appreciate one."

His gaze naturally shifted to Grace, curious of her approval.

Obvious surprise lit her eyes.

Why was she surprised? "Do you not think it a good idea, Miss Steele?"

"I . . . I do." A smile flashed across her mouth. "I think it's a grand idea."

Relief filled his lungs. He directed his carriage driver to the family who had recently recovered from having their home rebuilt. They were terribly gracious to him, thanking him for his aid in the reconstruction and for the silly kissing bough.

He had humored his sister over this ridiculous project, wanting to redeem himself for failing her as a brother, but now he appreciated her creative desire to serve her neighbors. By the third delivery, he was convinced that his sister had been inspired. Nothing had brought a feeling of connection to his tenants in the last fifteen months as did this one small act of kindness.

It was late afternoon by the time they completed their last delivery. All of them leaned back into the carriage with cheeks rosy from the cold and hearts lighter from the joy they had brought to the neighborhood.

"Shall we return to Belside Manor for melted chocolate and shortbread?" Bridget asked.

"Will it be Gracie's recipe?" Richard asked, his nickname for Grace slipping out before he realized it. His gaze whipped to Ruth's, who smiled smugly at her sister. Drat! Why had he put his foot in his mouth?

Grace met his eyes, understanding and assurance there. He had wanted to read her mind earlier, but she was reading his. "Of course, Gracie's famous chocolate will be served. Soon the fashionable houses in London will get wind of it and be begging for the recipe."

Just like that, she had smoothed out the situation, as if she had coined the nickname herself.

When they reached Belside manor, the staff was in full force turning out the house with Christmas decor. Bridget pointed to the ceiling. "I instructed them to hang our kissing bough under the entrance hall chandelier. I cannot wait to see it."

"Ours will be hung in the library." Grace unwrapped her scarf from her neck. "Since our parents take this tradition very seriously, and we prefer they steal their kisses behind closed doors."

They all laughed. Bridget was a whirlwind of energy, emboldened by their day, and was the first to cast off her outer clothing. She hurried to find a servant to request their chocolate and biscuits.

"All this day needs is a little music," Ruth said. "Mr. Graham, do you mind if I look through your sheet music?"

The direct question, without a hint of shyness, nearly stopped him in his tracks. "You need not ask. Make yourself at home." Home . . . if all went as planned, she would be the mistress here.

He gulped down the wave of regret building in his throat. Grace came up beside him, her hand coming to rest on his arm.

"She feels safe here. Ruth is only ever herself at home. You should be proud of your efforts. I believe she views you as a true friend now."

A friend. People had married less before.

"What's wrong?"

He shook his head. "I am glad she feels safe here. I want everyone to feel the same when at Belside. Shall we see what music she plans to play? Perhaps she will pick a song for you to sing."

"You know I am not musical."

He thought of the obnoxious requirement on Aunt's list. "You should learn."

"I fear it's too late for me."

"Nonsense. There is nothing like today." He slid his arm behind her back, as if it was the most natural place to rest it in the world, and led her to the drawing room. He released it just before they entered and missed the feel of her immediately.

The next hour was full of relaxed chatter and idle speculation on who would use the kissing boughs first at each house. Ruth played a few songs, and while Grace refused to sing, the afternoon was perfect. He was content to have time away from his problems. After all the chocolate was gone, Ruth announced her desire to return home.

As they walked into the entrance hall, Bridget shrieked, "There it is!" She pointed to the kissing bough hanging in all its red, white, and green glory. The smell of evergreen permeated every corner, seemingly wrapping them up in the holiday spirit.

"Of all the baskets we made, I believe this one is my favorite." Grace moved to look up at it.

Bridget grinned. "I might have selfishly saved the best for ourselves." She sighed with pleasure. "It is such a triumph seeing one's creation displayed like that."

Ruth put on her cloak. "All it needs is a willing couple."

Bridget's eyes widened. "Oh, yes. And fortunately, we have the perfect couple standing right beneath it." She motioned to him and Grace.

"Us?" Grace laughed a little hysterically, and every muscle in his body seemed to tighten. He looked at Grace and then up at the mistletoe they'd been appreciating. When had they positioned themselves beneath it?

"Come now," Ruth said. "It's just a little sporting fun, and Mr. Graham is a gentleman."

He cleared his throat. "I am a gentleman . . ."

"And it's tradition," Bridget added, moving to Ruth's side as if showing her allegiance in some unspoken battle. "There's nothing at all untoward about it."

He swallowed and turned to Grace.

She glowered up at him, but it didn't hide the array of emotions passing over her. "You wouldn't dare."

"Are you calling me a coward?"

"Not my words exactly, but I believe the description is adequate in this situation." That pert nose lifted in an air of superiority, but he caught the slightest tremble of her lips.

Oh, this was going to be fun. It felt like all the times they'd bantered before, but this time neither of them would have to run from the growing tension between them. He stepped closer, the toes of his boots touching the toes of her own. "When have I ever backed down from a challenge?"

She visibly swallowed. "You can become a coward at any moment, and today just happens to be your unlucky day."

He wanted to laugh at her logic. "And what about you? You're no coward?"

"Ha! I can handle a simple kiss. You think every woman swoons at your feet, but I assure you, I will not."

The gauntlet had been thrown. His voice dropped to a whisper. "Very well. Don't blame me if you cannot stop dreaming about me tonight." He knew what he'd be dreaming about, and he hadn't even touched her yet. The thought of remedying that, with full, guiltless permission, set his hands in motion. He circled her waist and drew her to him, her hands flying to rest at his chest.

"What are you doing?" she asked breathlessly.

"We're going to kiss, aren't we?" he whispered, not wanting to continue if she did not want it.

Her eyes darted to his. "That's only our lips touching, not the rest of us."

"Maybe if you're kissing Mr. Dobson. A real man isn't so inept." His words were brusque, but it was because she felt insanely comfortable in his arms, and he didn't know what to make of it.

She licked the corner of her mouth, unwittingly teasing his sensibilities. "Shan't I be the judge of your abilities?" she asked, blinking slowly.

Her sea-blue-green eyes drew him ever closer—the color bold, inviting. He looked at her for three counts, her breath on his mouth, the smell of her holding him captive, his blood rising and heat climbing, and then leaned forward and set his lips against hers. Instead of grazing her mouth as he had intended to do, he felt her challenge pushing him to make it at least a little memorable. A memory that would sustain him, should he never kiss her again.

He caught her bottom lip between his, moving his mouth against hers, careful at first and incredibly gentle. But Grace was no docile animal who would shirk a little touch and shy away. She was a clever fox who had enticed him with her mere smile, needling words, and loving heart. She leaned into him, catching him completely off guard, filling him with her scent, her heat, her passion. She kissed him back as if she were the expert—as if she intended to not just haunt his dreams forever but be in his every waking thought too.

Her hands slid up his chest and splayed half on his face and half his neck, sending a thrill through his body. Whatever power she was unleashing, he yearned for it. A hum filled his ears like his head was under water, drowning in perfection. His hands tightened around her silky gown. She had been his support, his partner, his joy these last weeks, and all his hidden, growing feelings he had fought to suppress were suddenly freed.

But this was Grace. His sister's friend. The woman who annoyed him to no end. And he was kissing her and forgetting every reason he shouldn't.

Belside. He forced the word into his mind. Belside. He had to think of Belside.

With all the willpower he could muster, he broke the kiss, his chest heaving.

She drew her own breath, her cheeks red, and her eyes glazed over. Her smile unfolded slowly like the petals of a flower.

Heavens, she was beautiful.

Grace. Was beautiful.

And she felt like heaven in his arms.

He was going to kill his sister.

Releasing Grace took effort, but he stepped back. He'd gone too far. Kissed her for too long. He turned. "Bridget, I . . ." But Bridget was nowhere in sight and neither was Ruth. The front door was ajar, sending a swirl of cold through its narrow gap, but he felt none of it. The warmth Grace had gifted him still clung to him like the softest blanket he'd ever touched.

He looked back at Grace, who ducked her head shyly. Did . . . did she care for him as much as he had come to care for her?

He swallowed, aching to pull her to him again.

They would never be able to return from this.

Not ever.

Chapter 18

GRACE STRUGGLED TO PAY attention to the Christmas Day sermon. The chapel overflowed with attendants coming to worship for the holiday, and it was the people who provided the greatest distraction to her. Mr. Craig, dressed in a very fine olive dress jacket, sat behind her with his sister, and she could feel his admiring stare on the back of her head. From what she had heard from her mother about his situation, he was from an upstanding family with ideal connections. He was not only available, but interested. And even more remarkable, she hadn't scared him off yet.

If she was smart, she would consider him.

But her wisdom had been commandeered by a fantasy that had begun yesterday afternoon after one remarkable mistletoe kiss. Admittedly, it *had* been her first kiss, so she had naught to compare it with, but shouldn't there have been charts in the Farmers' Almanac discussing the very complicated emotions produced while kissing under mistletoe? At the very least, the astrology section should have discussed how the very heavens seemed to have held their breath.

No wonder some thought it a heathen plant.

Although, she was quite certain such a light feeling was as divine as any. Even with such a conclusion, she had yet to decide if that feeling was meant to remain or act as a tormenting dream. Thinking of Richard had always been tormenting, so why should this be any different?

But it wasn't just his kiss. It had been him. The only thing separating her heart from his all these years was her utter conviction of the state of his character. Yesterday, he had proved her completely wrong. First with Miss Coleridge and then with his tenants. He had dipped his head humbly when they had spoken of their gratitude for all he had done for them.

Richard had thoroughly surprised her.

Her thoughts skipped down the bench past her sister, brother, and parents and crossed the aisle. Trailing up one bench more on the opposite side of them sat Richard and Bridget. Her eyes settled on Richard's handsome profile, her thoughts arresting on the subject of her desire. She could almost feel his jaw beneath her hands.

Some memories were unforgettable.

Kissing Richard Graham would always be one of them.

Richard turned at that moment and met her gaze head on. Her cheeks flooded with warmth, but she couldn't bring herself to look away. The smallest smile touched his lips and the way his almond eyes lifted upward at the corners gave her an unspoken answer to a question that had nagged at her all night and morning.

Had he regretted their kiss?

Nothing in his posture or expression gave her that impression. His smile continued to pull up on one side, and he nodded toward the vicar as if to say he was going to pay attention and she should as well.

He turned his head forward, breaking their silent connection. It was as if their roles had reversed. She would have scolded him in the past if he'd been distracted at church, and now he was the one paying attention and prompting her to do the same. He had grown up, while her mind was a child's toy ship without navigation.

Ruth elbowed her. "Stop staring or you'll be the subject of gossip at everyone's dinner table tonight."

Her head shifted forward. She did not want to add any more gossip than what would happen naturally when Richard proposed marriage to Ruth. Which he should have already done by now. His time was running out. But did he still care for Ruth? Because she suddenly wanted him to care for her . . .

After the sermon ended, Ruth slipped away to play soft organ music while everyone exited their pews and departed into the brisk weather. Grace's small frame allowed her to pass her brother by, and her parents, in her haste to leave first. However, she had not been prepared for Mrs. Cottswater, the vicar's wife, to approach her. Good heavens. That woman could prattle a person's life away.

Grace stepped right in front of her willowy figure and managed to open her mouth first. "Have you met the Craigs who are visiting?"

"No, I have not. I always love to greet our town's visitors and invite them to dinner."

"I will introduce you." She turned just as the Petersons left their pew, allowing the Craigs to leave next.

"Miss Steele," Mr. Craig said. "I was hoping to speak to you."

"Mr. Craig, Miss Craig, how do you do? I have an introduction to make. Everyone in Wetherfield must make the acquaintance of Mrs. Cottswater." She finished the introduction just as Bridget reached her side. The timing couldn't have been better. "Will you excuse me? I had promised to speak to Miss Graham."

Mrs. Cottswater did just as Grace hoped and caught Mr. Craig's and his sister's arm and began telling them all about the history of the church building. If she knew her well, Mrs. Cottswater wouldn't stop until she reviewed the lives of the last seven vicars.

Bridget linked arms with her. "We have so much to talk about." She looked behind her to allow Grace to see her father speaking to Richard. They often greeted each other, but she knew Bridget's pointed stare was only for her brother. She wanted to know about their kiss.

"Not in the church!" Grace whispered. "Later."

Bridget shook her head. "Tobias has already run off to meet up with the Gilbert boys, and your mother will be in conversation with Mrs. Gardener for an age. Let's speak in your carriage until they're ready to leave."

"What about *your* brother?"

"I cannot predict how long he'll speak to your father, but I'm willing to risk his annoyance for this very important conversation."

"Very well, but we had better walk fast." She didn't want to risk being pulled back into the conversation with the Craigs and Mrs. Cottswater.

As soon as they were outside, Bridget's questions began again. "Well, did he propose?"

Grace gave a high-pitched laugh. "No, and save this mortifying interview for the privacy of the carriage, if you please."

With hurried steps, they reached her family's carriage and climbed inside. Once the door was shut, Bridget sighed. "Finally. Now tell me everything! Are we to be sisters?"

How to answer? Grace leaned back into the firm upholstery. "There are no plans for an engagement. It was just a kiss—a forced kiss—if you remember."

"Ruth and I slipped outside as soon as you started kissing. If my brother was not proposing, what took so long?"

She couldn't tell Bridget that their kiss was what had taken so long. It felt too private, like something she and Richard ought to treasure alone. Which was strange because if she had something to share, she generally wanted it to be with Bridget. "May I ask why you expected Richard to propose? Did he say something to you that led you to believe that?"

Bridget fell back against the opposite seat. "No, he didn't. Not exactly. But his actions, his attention to you, it all painted a very clear picture of his intentions."

"Didn't I tell you that he was interested in Ruth?" Even saying such words hurt.

Bridget sat up again in a rush. "You cannot still be on about that nonsense. While you're endeavoring to get Ruth by Richard's side, I'm striving equally hard to keep her away from you two. We really need to be united on this."

Grace's brow wrinkled in confusion. "Wait, you're trying to keep her away?"

"Honestly, Grace. You have done impressively well with your tactics to bring Ruth into the picture, but you need to stop being a martyr and see to your own heart. It's not Ruth I see as my brother's equal, it's you."

Was that even possible? She glanced through the window and caught sight of her mother walking to the carriage with Ruth and Tobias by her side. Just behind them, she spotted her father with Richard. They didn't have much more time alone in the carriage, but her gaze couldn't pull away from Richard. He smiled at something Father said. She used to get instantly irritated when she saw that smile. Its perfect curve and those straight teeth were better fit for a portrait in the gallery than someone with real feelings. But now she saw his smile and wondered what had caused it, and if she could do something to make it stay forever.

She knew his heart better and that he was more than a pleasant face to admire who sought others' happiness before his own. What was wrong with her? Even as she asked herself the question, she knew the answer. "Good heavens, Bridget. You're right. Richard can't marry Ruth."

Bridget gave a short laugh. "I know. That's what I have been telling you."

Grace ripped her gaze from the window to meet Bridget's confident one. "What am I going to do?"

"What do you mean?"

"I mean, I'm beginning to care for that vexing man." Panic built at a rapid pace. What if he had been speaking to her father about Ruth? She couldn't stand between him and Belside. But what did she do with these overwhelming feelings?

Bridget clapped as she always did when she was excited. "You have to tell him."

She adamantly shook her head, the pins in her hair loosening. "I don't have to do anything of the sort."

"Grace, you are my dearest friend, so I am going to be honest with you. You're a beautiful, charming woman who has a tendency to chase away any suitor who shows interest in you. If you truly love my brother, I cannot let you do the same to him."

Grace and Bridget had always been frank with each other, but even though Grace knew this about herself, having Bridget say it out loud struck a painful chord inside her. She did chase men away. And she was good at it. Bridget had been all the companionship she needed until recently, and no one else had made her feel anything—except Richard. She had mistaken her flustered response to him as something she must avoid at all costs. She had been keeping Richard at arm's length for her entire life, and she didn't know how to suddenly stop doing that.

"Bridget, I cannot simply—"

"There's more," Bridget interrupted. "Not only do you chase away your suitors, you chase away Richard's too. For years, if you've discovered a woman interested in Richard, or vice versa, you've chased them away too."

It was easy enough to recall her efforts to dissuade Miss Harrington, exaggerating how poorly Richard danced, interrupting their conversations and pushing other men her way. She had been less overt with Miss Thorne, but the conclusion had been the same. It wasn't merely for Bridget's sake as she had previously justified. It bothered her seeing him with other women. Good gracious, what was wrong with her?

Bridget seemed to guess her internal question. "Can't you see, you have been in love with Richard for much longer than today."

Grace couldn't do anything more than blink. "Upon my word, I'm a terrible person." She had been contemplating throwing herself between Richard and Ruth.

"Nonsense. You are devoted to those you care for, but when it comes to men—Richard specifically—you will have to adjust your plan of attack."

"Must I attack? Such phrasing produces results, but not the kind I want. I won't ruin Richard's happiness this time. If he is meant to be with Ruth . . ." She couldn't finish her sentence because she did not believe it to be true.

"He is meant to be with the person he cares for in return, and the only way to discover this is to have a frank conversation about it."

"A very mature strategy." No scheming. No running away.

"I thought so too." Bridget pulled on the ends of her gloves. "I plan to have a frank conversation with my mother too, when she returns. It's high time she lets me attend balls."

Grace nodded. "You are braver than I."

Bridget shook her head. "You are going to be my inspiration. Once you do it, I will have the courage too. Which is why you have to tell him straightaway."

"How? When?"

"Come for Christmas dinner tonight, and we'll create a way for you to get him alone." Before Grace could answer, Bridget swung open the carriage door. "And don't mince words! Kiss him again if you have to."

"What?"

But it was too late. Grace's family had come and Bridget was moving to join her brother. Richard tipped his hat to her in a silent greeting.

She couldn't respond for fear that she would blurt out how Bridget thought they should kiss again. And what did he think about it?

Good heavens, maybe she should confess before she lost her dignity and did something even more foolish.

Chapter 19

RICHARD MADE HIS WAY to his study after breakfast, ready to review his correspondence again. He had stayed up to the wee hours looking over an investment opportunity his solicitor had sent him. It held great risk. He would have to mortgage the house, but the outcome would have the potential to pay off his debts and more so. He would never have considered anything so drastic before, but never had things been so complicated.

The week before Christmas, he had tried hard to take every opportunity to speak with Ruth, to be near her. Many of those moments had been provided to him by Grace as they went to town for more supplies, trekked through the woods for holly berries, and added finishing touches to the kissing boughs. He had made progress in getting to know his quiet neighbor, but his feelings had progressed in a completely different direction.

Grace.

They teased each other and made each other laugh. She challenged him and listened too. She was beginning to be the first person he thought of when he woke and the last before he fell asleep. He had only studied the investment opportunity so he could be free to court her. Hoping beyond measure that he could forget Aunt's inheritance and court Grace in earnest.

He didn't know if she would even welcome his attention, should such a miracle change his circumstances, but he couldn't help letting his mind linger on it. She still goaded him and urged him to be better, and he still teased her in return, but had he imagined the shift between them? He wished he could have a single glimpse into her mind to examine her innermost thoughts. Would he find himself there? Was it worth risking all of Belside and his family's happiness on such a question?

Just after entering his study, his butler presented him a letter.

He glanced at it and immediately recognized the handwriting.

It was from Mother.

Her last letter had been posted shortly after she had arrived in Bath and had not been a positive one. He dreaded hearing that she had somehow worsened because of the trip. He broke the seal and unfolded the paper.

Dearest Richard,

I am writing this letter to set you at ease and tell you how much I am enjoying myself. You might not believe me, but it is true. Bath has been full of pleasant surprises! We have been invited to dine with friends three times this week. As you know, I resented you and Bridget for being so eager for me to leave your side, but I am grateful to you now. The company tires me, but not because my spirits are poor. Indeed, it is because I have little to converse about. Over a year of mourning has turned me into a dull companion. I am rallying though, day by day, and I feel stronger than ever. Now all I can think about is my desire to return to Belside. Being here makes me long for it. I cannot truly enjoy anything without wanting to share it with my children.

Thinking of you always,

Mother

A sigh of relief sang from his lips. She was doing better. Guilt quickly followed his sigh. Mother longed for Belside.

He shoved the letter into his waistcoat pocket to remind him to send a reply. He was not in the mindset to do so now. Just the mention of the house and estate drained his energy. He pulled the calendar to him, not needing to count to know how much time he had left—not enough. The lines between the dates were unbendable prison bars, holding him captive to the rules of time. If he was going to marry Ruth, he needed to propose. Tonight. But how could he do so? It was Grace who consumed his thoughts when they were apart. Grace who challenged him to be better. And Grace who made his pulse race at the mere sight of her.

He'd hardly heard a word at church, though he had tried. She was all he could think about.

A second sigh slipped through his lips. They'd created a mess between them, confusing the family and confusing each other. And it was all *her* fault. A half smile slid over his mouth with the mere thought of her meeting his gaze in church yesterday. She had already woven herself into his family's hearts, and through goading him, she had secured herself in his too.

She'd ruin everything.

And he wanted her to.

He sat back in his chair and let his gaze wander to the window. In losing Belside, it would save him. Save him from sacrificing his future for his family. She would give him back a chance to have love in his life. But if he chose Grace, he would lose everything else, and so would his family.

He needed advice. Grace would know what to do.

Grace?

How was he supposed to ask her?

He stood, massaging his tired eyes. He needed a nap before dinner. Surely, a little more sleep would help him see reason. Too tired to climb the stairs for dinner, he made his way to the dining room and sprawled out across the sofa.

Chapter 20

GRACE SHOULD HAVE BEEN with her family for Christmas dinner, but as soon as she had mentioned Bridget's invitation to Mama, she had practically been thrown out the door. After, of course, she had been subjected to Mama's particular fussing over her hair and dress. She even bore a hint of rouge on her cheeks and a lip salve colored with saffron. She felt almost as decorated as the houses for the holiday.

"What do we do about a chaperone?" Mama worried, while she studied Grace's reflection at her dressing table.

Grace wrinkled her nose. "Chaperone? At Belside? I have never required one before."

"Yes, but that was before Mr. Graham began courting you."

"I wouldn't call it courting," she argued. "We have barely established a friendship." Her feelings said otherwise, but there was nothing official for Mama to be concerned about. It was Belside they were speaking about. Her second home!

"Nonetheless," Mama began again. "If you were to become engaged to Mr. Graham, I wouldn't want anyone to discover you had visited there these last weeks without a chaperone."

Engaged. The word suddenly carried tangible weight.

"I cannot miss Christmas dinner with Mr. Steele, but I do want you to go." Mama snapped her fingers. "I shall send Ruth with you."

"Ruth?" It wasn't the worst option, but would her sister's presence remind Richard of his previous desire to marry her? She pushed the concern from her mind. All she required was a moment alone to share her feelings with Richard. Then come what may.

Ruth went along with the plan, and soon the carriage was pulling them both in front of Belside. Cloaked in a night's winter scene that nearly stole her breath away, the manor stood in frosted glory. Despite the biting temperature, there was nothing cold about the picture in front of her. Lines of snow on the eaves and smoke curling from the chimneys made the large edifice appear cozy and inviting.

"Oh, dear." Ruth set her gloved hand on her head. "I daresay my headache has worsened."

"What headache?" Grace shifted her gaze and squinted in the dark to see her sister clearer.

"The one I had before we left, which now feels like the pulse of a beast. I apologize, but I must return home to bed."

"I won't ask about that analogy, but of course, you must return home. It was silly to come here for Christmas dinner at all."

"Nonsense," Ruth said. "You must stay. We cannot both return home."

"You are my chaperone, remember?" Grace stuck the finger of her glove between her teeth. It would not take long to speak to Richard. She did not have to stay for dinner. "I wonder if you could return home and then send the carriage back for me. I will stay long enough to make my apologies, and then return home again."

Ruth lowered her hand. "If that is what you wish. I am sorry to ruin your evening."

"Not at all." She wished her sister better and climbed down from the carriage. By the time she reached the doorstep, the conveyance departed behind her, and there was no turning back. She knocked and waited, shivering and constantly flipping obnoxious curls away from her face.

What would she say to Richard? How did she confess her feelings to a man she had spent years criticizing?

"I hadn't meant for it to happen . . ." She shook her head. No, that sounded like an apology. That was not what she wanted. "It wasn't your appearance, so don't let this feed your vanity." Good heavens. Did she plan to chase him away too? She desired to be direct and concise. Flustered, she shouted into the wind the confession she wished to make. "Just kiss me again, will you?"

The door swung open as she belted the words. The butler's eyes widened.

She winced. "Those were, er, lines to a play." She ducked inside, wishing she could toss out the tree in the corner and use the empty flower pot to cover her flaming cheeks.

If only life was so convenient.

"Where might I find Miss Graham?" Her voice squeaked out the words.

The butler accepted her cloak. "Miss Graham is changing for dinner and said to wait for her in the drawing room."

"Excellent," she muttered. She hurried past him, her hand casually shielding her eyes from his. She rubbed her icy hands together, chastising herself with every step toward the drawing room. Once inside, she moved straight to the warm fire crackling behind the grate. Not five feet from the fire, her feet suddenly stopped. There was Richard prostrate on the sofa and fast asleep.

Was he ill?

She forgot all about the chill she'd taken outside and hurried to his side.

"Richard?"

His eyes did not so much as flutter open and his entire form held eerily still. She hastily removed one glove and reached to set her hand on his forehead to see if he had succumbed to a fever. An inch from his skin she hesitated. Her pulse began to pound in her chest. If she woke him, she would have to tell him her secret.

But that was why she was here, wasn't it?

Was she ready?

She shook her head. If he were ill, he needed assistance. That is what mattered at the moment. As slowly and carefully as she dared, she set a few fingers against his skin. Warmth radiated there, but not the powerful heat of a fever. Her shoulders dropped and relief soared through her. She had never known Richard to sleep during the day, but at least he was healthy.

She lightly brushed his forehead as she removed her hand and let it drop to her side. Now what? She studied his handsome face, trying to decide if she should run back home or wake him and get it over with.

Tilting her head, she admired the lines of his cheekbone down to his jaw. Maybe it *was* his appearance that started her feelings for him. He was so very nice to look at. Glancing over her shoulder to assure Bridget was not yet there, she lowered herself to her knees for a better look. Why not? This might be her only chance to do so. If he rejected her and married her sister, she would probably try to never look at him again . . . ever. How else would she be able to control her increasing attraction to him?

She would just admire him for a moment and then she would wake him and . . . and . . . her train of thought waned as her eyes wandered to his mouth. She found herself leaning toward him. What if she kissed him while he slept? Just in case that could never happen again too. With her glove in her fist, she set her hand carefully on his shoulder and dipped her head.

She was mere inches away when Richard's eyes cracked open.

"Gracie?" he whispered.

Her limbs became paralyzed with shock, and she couldn't answer him.

His brows lowered. "Am I dreaming?"

"Yes," she blurted, on impulse.

"Good." His arm came up around her back, and she couldn't breathe. And then with a gentle pull, he drew her closer.

A loud thud sounded from behind them, the door hitting the wall. "What in the name of all that is good and holy is happening here?" The exclamation behind them set Richard leaping off the sofa. Grace jumped in fright too, but not so elegantly, and her head hit Richard's chest. He caught her arm and stepped on her toe. After a moment, they managed to stand side by side, chests heaving, while they stared at who had caught them in a most compromising position.

The older woman had straight, imposing shoulders beneath her purple muslin gown. Her gray hair sat perfectly coiffed atop her head as if a single hair did not risk the woman's ire by being out of place. But most notable of all was her very scandalized expression.

"Aunt Edith," Richard gaped. "What are you doing here?"

"Saving the family name, apparently." She tapped a cane on the ground for emphasis. Grace could not tell if she required the cane or if it was an affectation she used to intimidate people.

"It's not what you think," Richard said, holding up his hands.

Grace nodded her agreement because she hadn't quite found her voice yet. Nothing had happened, but she *had* been about to let Richard kiss her if he so desired. She wasn't about to admit to such a thing though.

"Oh?" his aunt said, pursing her wrinkled lips. "Is that why you have a woman's glove across your chest?"

Grace's head flung to see, and sure enough, her glove was draped across Richard as if stamping him with her touch.

He quickly removed it and handed it back to her. It was hers and there was no hiding the fact, so she reluctantly accepted it.

It was her turn to say something. "Forgive me, I found Mr. Graham asleep on the sofa when I arrived, and I was ascertaining if he was ill."

"He looks robust and healthy to me." His aunt's snippy voice sent a dart of shame at her chest.

"Yes, he does, doesn't he?" she sighed heavily. Too healthy, if you asked her.

"Aunt, this is Miss Grace Steele. Miss Steele, my aunt, Lady Edith Walker."

After Grace dipped a curtsy, Richard abandoned her. He strode to his aunt's side. "Now that you know it was a complete misunderstanding, you must sit down and rest." He took her arm and led her into the room.

Lady Edith sniffed. "I suppose I should. I am dying, you know."

Grace could not believe her blunt manners, but Richard took them in stride.

"Which is why I am utterly surprised to find you have traveled all this way," he said.

"I am making the rounds and saying my good-byes." Effortlessly taking her seat as if she had never been sick a day in her life, Lady Edith swung her gaze to meet Grace's. Lifting her cane, she pointed it at her. "Is this the woman you have engaged yourself to?"

Grace squirmed in her chair.

Richard cleared his throat before answering. "No, I am not engaged at present."

His aunt made a high-pitched noise. "Not engaged? Did you read my letter?"

"Both of them, yes."

Grace's eyes went back and forth between the two of them, wishing she was anywhere else in the world, but also completely fascinated by the unnerving conversation.

"And have you even found a woman of my liking?"

Of *her* liking? What was that supposed to mean?

Richard shot Grace a glance. "I have, but might we speak of this in the morning? Dinner should be ready soon, and as you can see, we have a guest present."

Lady Edith gave an elegant snort of derision. Grace did not know how she managed it, but she did. "Guest?" she said. "Is that what you call this heathen girl?"

Grace scowled and squeezed her hands in her lap to keep from shooting a biting remark. "I cannot stay. My chaperone had a headache and returned already. I came inside to make my apologies and wish the family goodnight before returning myself."

Lady Edith drew a fan from her reticule and began beating the air by her face. "No chaperone? This story grows worse by the second."

Richard's voice grew tight. "Miss Steele is our closest neighbor and a dear friend to both Bridget and myself. She has my highest respect. Despite what you saw, I must plead with you to see the innocence in it."

His firm words softened Grace's anger considerably. In fact, they melted her very soul. His *highest* respect? Her?

"Aunt Edith!" Bridget called from the door. "What on earth are you doing here? Shouldn't you be home in bed?" She rushed into the room to her aunt's side and kissed her cheek.

"Yes, yes. Sit down, Bridget. Your energy tires me out."

Bridget rushed to Grace's side and took a seat beside her.

"Where have you been?" Grace asked through her clenched teeth.

"Giving you time to confess," she whispered back.

Grace squeezed Bridget's hand to communicate her feelings on that regard. The woman who had the potential to save Belside from financial ruin was sitting across from her, and Grace had made the worst possible first impression. Richard's aunt would never let him marry her in exchange for money.

"Miss Steele," Richard said, clearing his throat. "Now that my aunt is here, certainly you can dine with us without any concern of propriety."

Leaving seemed the smartest course of action, but Richard's eyes begged her to stay. She hesitated, but when Bridget nodded furiously at her, she relented. If they both wanted her here, certainly she could bear their aunt's derision for one night. "I suppose I can send a quick note to Callis Hall to inform my parents of the change of circumstance."

Richard gave a nod that seemed laced with meaning. Relief? Gratitude? She could not say what.

Dinner was announced and Richard led his aunt out of the room. Bridget held Grace back. "What happened? My aunt is glaring daggers at you."

Richard did not so much as glance back at her. "I might have ruined everything."

Bridget linked arms with her. "That sounds dramatic, especially coming from you. Just fix it like you always do."

Could she redeem herself? What sort of mad plan could she enact over dinner to undo the last hour? Her mind went blank. If she was going to do something, the time was now. But no ready solution presented itself. Was her cleverness dried up? Is that what love did to a person?

Chapter 21

AUNT EDITH CLUTCHED RICHARD'S arm with a surprisingly tight grip for an aged, sick woman. "There is nothing I like worse than a scandal, Richard."

"They're nasty things, aren't they?" He patted her hand while simultaneously leading her to her seat at the table. He had to remain calm if he were to convince his aunt, but the truth was, he *had* been found in a very compromising position.

"Don't placate me. I wasn't born yesterday. I don't like that *Miss Steele*. She has a mischievous look about the eyes." Aunt Edith waved her hand in front of her face for emphasis.

She wasn't wrong about that look. Richard knew it well. "If you give her a chance, I promise you will wonder how you ever got on without her." His lips pulled up on one side as Grace walked into the room arm in arm with Bridget. She had certainly grown on him over the last month. Indeed, he wouldn't mind knowing her even better.

He had thought he had been dreaming when he had opened his eyes from his nap, and if Aunt Edith had walked in a moment later, he would have kissed her. All his hope for Belside would have been lost.

He would have been made to marry Grace to save her reputation.

He was almost disappointed it hadn't come to that. He wouldn't have minded kissing Grace again or facing the consequence of his choices. What did that say about him? That he was selfish? Wasn't that what Grace hated about him? Maybe he hadn't changed at all.

Once they were all seated, the first course was served. Silence hovered about the table. He tried not to look at Grace so his aunt would not make a fuss, but he discreetly stole a glance at her to see how she was faring.

She seemed to sense his gaze, and she looked up at him. Her appearance was altered—more color in her cheeks and soft curls framing her face—but it was her worried eyes that concerned him.

His aunt could be difficult to deal with. How he longed to reassure her and beg her not to fret about what had happened, but he couldn't console her just yet. Doing the next best thing, he communicated the only way he could think to do and winked at her.

The lines of her face softened and the smallest smile played on her lips. To his surprise, she reassured him and winked back.

Aunt inhaled sharply. "What is this? Only *light-skirts* wink at a man. And at the dinner table, no less. I am quite appalled."

Bridget snorted, causing her to choke on her food. She coughed a few times into her napkin.

Richard tried not to laugh, and the only thing that kept him from doing so was seeing the horror on Grace's face. He had never seen her so thoroughly embarrassed.

"Miss Steele never winks," he said quickly. "She must have something in her eye. Does she not deserve our sympathy?"

"Is that true, Miss Steele?" Aunt skewered her with a look that could turn a creature to stone.

A forced smile crossed Grace's mouth and she answered glibly. "I must have been overcome with this delightful Christmas fare and stared too long without blinking."

Aunt's frown deepened. "The Christmas fare, so you say? Perhaps you were staring too long and hard at my nephew."

It was Grace's turn to choke. Her sharp inhale led to a cough, which was silenced by a long drink of water. Richard jumped in to save her. "Miss Steele reminds me frequently that I am not as handsome as I think I am. I assure you, she would not stare overlong at me."

Aunt raised a suspicious brow, but his words seemed to do the trick. Grace avoided looking at him through the rest of the second course. His hand fiddled with his fork, not certain what to do. His eyes passed frequently to his aunt, who seemed to eat everything in sight and devoured a whole leg of Christmas goose. She gleamed with continued hunger when the dessert was served with all the pomp and fuss of a celebratory meal: Christmas tourte a la Chatelaine filled with plums, cherries, and currants, with a glazed crust topped with toasted almonds.

"Aunt, can you tell me about your illness?" Richard hedged.

"It isn't proper dinner conversation," she said, dabbing her lips with her napkin. "But it's cancer of the stomach. A wretched disease that gives me such pains in my side and fluttering through my middle. The doctors tell me I do not have much time left."

Richard blinked several times, a little worried about his aunt's mental state. "Should you be eating so much then?"

"Do you wish to deprive me of what could be my last meal?" She tsked her tongue. "It hurts no matter what I consume, so I don't intend to look like a withered tree in my casket."

"I am sorry to hear you've been suffering," Grace said carefully.

"I had no idea," Bridget added. "And you traveled all this way."

Aunt dipped her hand in her finger glass beside her plate. "When a person is driven with purpose, life's obstacles are more of a hindrance than a barricade."

Richard could not believe it. She had come all this way just to ensure he married before she died. What other purpose could she be speaking of?

After everyone had finished their dessert, Richard forwent his port and retired to the sitting room with the ladies. His mind was all but consumed with the puzzle concerning his future. The pieces did not fit together. Not Ruth. Not Aunt's will. Not saving Belside. But Grace . . . she was a piece he had not let himself try yet. He had a feeling that if he did, she would slide together next to him with perfect ease.

He took a seat next to his aunt and searched her countenance for signs of fatigue. "Are you certain you would not like to lie down after your journey?"

"Nonsense. I have plenty of energy for a little entertainment."

Entertainment? Richard grimaced. After a Christmas feast, everyone was generally too full to do much more than visit. As for him, his mind was full of an abundance of thoughts and worries.

"What about a game?" Grace asked. "I could think of a few that Lady Edith might enjoy."

"No, I detest games," Aunt said, curling her lip in disgust. "When I come to Belside, I expect music. Bridget, why don't you play for us?"

Bridget sent Grace an apologetic glance and disappeared behind the pianoforte. If Grace would look at him, he might send her one equally sorry, but she was still avoiding his gaze. Bridget's fingers effortlessly played "While Shepherds Watched Their Flocks at Night," reminding Richard of how impressive her talent was. He didn't always notice such things about his sister.

Aunt Edith pointed to Grace next. "Now it's your turn, Miss Steele. What will you play?"

Richard stilled, waiting to see how Grace would react.

Grace's smile immediately set him at ease. Bless that woman for being made of thicker stuff than most. "I do not play, Lady Edith."

Aunt Edith frowned. "Then you can sing while Bridget plays."

"I do not think your ears would appreciate my poor abilities. However, I do blend well enough in a group. Shall we sing a carol together? 'Hark the Herald Angels Sing'?"

"An excellent idea." Richard stood before his aunt could object like she had to the suggestion of games. "Come, Aunt. I know how well you sing. You must join us." He set out his arm for her to take.

Aunt heaved a sigh. "If we must."

They gathered around the piano, with Bridget poised at the keys. He discreetly stepped between Grace and his aunt, hoping he could act as a barrier in more ways than one.

As the music began, they all began singing. His aunt had a rich alto voice, but it was hard to hear over the excited way Grace belted out the music. For such a small little pixie, she had a remarkable set of lungs. And she was right. She couldn't sing.

She couldn't blend either.

When Grace looked at him in the middle of "Hark the Herald Angels Sing," her broad grin made him laugh. She was thoroughly enjoying herself, despite the abysmal treatment she had received from his aunt. He didn't care if she couldn't carry a tune, he loved her.

He loved her.

The thought made him smile all the wider. He didn't know much about love, but if there was a defining emotion, this had to be it—a simultaneous increase of happiness, along with a settling peace. And more than anything, a tug he could barely resist toward the beautiful woman at his side.

This was how he wanted to celebrate all his Christmases. When Aunt tried to sit out the second song, he insisted they sing another.

He didn't push for a third, knowing she was likely worn to pieces, but he wished he could have. There was something special about singing the songs about Christ, and even more when surrounded by his family and Grace. He wished Mother had been there to have been a part of it. She would have loved it.

After the singing, they had a tedious conversation where Aunt pelted Grace with questions about philosophy and the great poets. Grace was not uneducated, and her comments were smart and witty, but they were not bookish enough to please his aunt. After every comment she made, Aunt Edith would give him a disapproving glance.

When the evening was drawing to a close, Aunt Edith complained of her stomach ailing her and insisted he take her to bed while Bridget saw their guest to the door. After seeing Aunt had everything she needed in her bedchamber, he returned downstairs, surprised to discover Bridget and Grace still in the entrance hall. Upon seeing him, Bridget made an excuse and left them alone. He had a feeling Aunt would suddenly descend on them from upstairs and set off a second cry of alarm.

"I thought I might have missed saying goodnight," he said to Grace.

She smiled. "Bridget's apologies were long-winded. I think she was hoping you would return before I left."

"I'm glad she kept you here. My aunt can be . . . a lot. But you weathered the evening like a brave soldier. I was impressed you did not desert us. Please tell me you weren't rattled too much."

"A little," she admitted. "But mostly because I know what her visit must mean for you."

"It could mean everything." He shrugged. "But I would rather talk about something less foreboding. You, for example. I was remiss in telling you how lovely you look tonight."

In the dim light, her cheeks were already a rosy hue, but her eyes rounded. "I do try a little harder on Christmas."

"Oh? Here I was hoping you were trying for me."

She laughed, but he swore she looked a tad guilty. "Is that what you think?" She quickly wrapped her cloak over her shoulders and tucked her gloved hands beneath the folds. "It's late, and I am sure my carriage is ready. Thank you for letting me join your Christmas dinner."

He nodded, stepping forward to cut off her escape. "Thank you for visiting my dreams."

Her eyes drew all the wider and her mouth fell open. "I was just . . . you were just . . ."

He chuckled, loving the way she reacted to him. "I know, Gracie. No harm done."

She clamped her mouth shut only to open it again a moment later. "There is something I need to speak to you about."

He inched closer. "I need to speak to you too."

She nibbled her bottom lip. "When?"

He tried not to stare at it. When was a good question. Aunt would not like him disappearing from her sight when she so rarely visited. But this was important too. "Tomorrow? Shall I call on you?"

"We'll never get a moment alone."

"Oh? You want to be alone with me?" He couldn't resist a smug, thoroughly satisfied smile.

She threw her gaze to the ceiling. "You're impossible."

He gently touched the edge of her cloak by her arm, coming as close as he dared to her. "Impossible does seem to be the reigning word today, but there are only two small letters to remove to make the word possible. Don't you have any faith in me?"

Her smile slowly returned, her voice serious. "More than I used to."

He savored the words. "That's progress already."

She didn't look away, and it nearly killed him that he had to send her home at all. Finally, she lowered her gaze to the floor. "Will you be coming to propose to Ruth? I should like to prepare myself."

Ruth? He had momentarily forgotten about Grace's sister or that she would be there when he came. His smile drooped. "No. Not tomorrow." He wanted to tell her that he would never propose to her sister, but the words would not come.

She nodded, and the lines by her eyes softened as if she understood what he could not say. "Goodnight, Richie."

"Goodnight, Gracie."

Chapter 22

GRACE LAY IN HER bed during that stage between wakefulness and sleeping. It was in this clear state, where the mind was not bogged down with tasks and conversation, where Grace remembered something from Mr. Green's Christmas ball. It was a riddle Richard had wanted her to solve in which she found him a single woman who was well-read, observant, mildly pretty, and exceptionally musical.

She had answered Ruth.

And not a day later, he had announced his intention to marry her.

Her eyes opened with sudden clarity. Did Richard *have* to marry Ruth, or someone like her, to save Belside? She pulled herself up on her elbows. Could it be a coincidence? Why had she not seen it before? The events of the previous night flooded into her mind. His Aunt Edith had been very particular about Grace. Could she have been particular about who she wanted Richard to marry too?

"Good heavens!" she said into the stillness of the room. What a terrible expectation for a relative to require, even if it was in exchange for money. She flipped the blanket off her legs and yanked the bellpull for her maid.

While she dressed, she fretted over the conclusion she had come to. She needed to clarify the whole situation with Richard. But deep down, a pit formed in her stomach. She had wanted Richard to turn his feelings to her, but what if that was not even an option?

And to think she had almost kissed him again last night and ruined everything for him. By the time breakfast was over, she was nearly convinced of his aunt's cruelty. She chewed on her fingernail, which she never did, when she was supposed to be sorting through all her clothes to donate for St. Stephen's Day. She managed a small pile, but she couldn't concentrate to manage anything greater.

Mama stuck her head into her bedchamber. "I finally have a moment to myself, and I want you to tell me all about last night."

This was not the time for Mama's excessive questions or hints of weddings. But she had to say something or Mama would not leave her alone. Where to start? "The food was excellent."

Mama came and sat down on the edge of her bed. "And?" Her wide expectant eyes were almost laughable.

"And we sang carols."

Mama's face lit up. "How lovely. . . Wait, did you sing too?"

"Of course. Carols are meant to be sung as a group."

Mama's smile drooped. "But you were not overly loud, were you?"

What a question. "We were singing praises, which are meant to be done with gusto."

"I see." Mama rubbed a spot on the center of her forehead.

Grace knew her voice was not the kind to be admired, but last night singing with Bridget and Richard had been wonderful. They did not care about the quality of her tone. They were her friends. She nearly smiled at that. She honestly counted Richard as her friend and a dear friend at that. They had come so far.

A maid interrupted them, announcing Mr. Craig had come to visit.

"Mr. Craig?" she repeated. No, no, no. Richard was supposed to visit, not Mr. Craig.

"Let's not keep him waiting," Mama said, waving her hand to get Grace to hurry. "Mr. Graham hasn't proposed yet, so you must keep your options open."

"Mama!" she chided.

Mama shrugged. "Not all courtships are about romance, you know. You have to think practically too."

Grace had always been practical, but she no longer wanted to be. She wanted the feeling that only came when Richard was near. But Mama was right. After the revelation Grace had come to this morning, Richard might be as unattainable as ever. She should be *very* nice to Mr. Craig. Although her heart would not be in it, she would try. She didn't want to be the woman Bridget had described her to be—the one who only chased away men.

Mr. Craig was overly charming during his visit. His eagerness and confidence led her to believe that he had a list of conquests at home. He complimented her in every other sentence, which made everything he said feel ungenuine. There was nothing unlikeable about him, but nothing likable either.

Mr. Craig discreetly shifted closer and closer until there was no longer a separate cushion between them on the sofa. Mama pulled out her knitting and turned her body away from them to allow a bit of privacy. Mr. Craig took it as an opportunity to press his leg against the outside of hers. Instead of a thrill, she felt a wave of unease.

He spoke to her in a lowered voice. "I am leaving after Twelfth Night, Miss Steele, but I would like to come again before the end of January. Would you welcome such a visit?"

This was her chance. She could secure his affection now and not have to leave Wetherfield. One thought persisted above the rest: He's not Richard.

"Forgive me," she said at last. "There is someone else my heart belongs to." Her face burned as she admitted the difficult words. But no matter how hard she had tried during his visit, she would never see herself with Mr. Craig. And it would not be fair to encourage him to ride such a far distance from his home if she could not return his affections.

His face went from surprised to disappointed, but he quickly masked it with a false smile. "I see. Is there an understanding between you and this man?"

"No."

He studied her for a moment. "But your heart is committed to him?"

She swallowed and gave a slow nod.

Their butler stepped in the room and announced the arrival of Mr. Graham.

Her breath caught in anticipation. He had come. Finally!

Richard stepped into the room like a man straight from a fashion magazine, his smile alone made her want to take up painting to remember it forever. His eyes scanned the room, stopping on her.

And then his smile reached his eyes, stopping her heart in the process.

But when it reached Mr. Craig, it dropped a good two notches. "I hope I am not interrupting," he said.

Mr. Craig looked between the two of them and sighed. "Not at all. It seems my time here has come to an end."

"Good," Richard said. "I mean, it was good to see you again."

Mr. Craig stood. "I certainly hope so. For me, it has been a pleasure." He dipped his head to Mrs. Steele and Richard before turning back to her, dropping his voice yet again. "If it had been anyone less worthy, I might not have given up so easily."

She almost laughed in surprise. Mr. Craig had known without her saying anything more. Had her feelings been so obvious? "I thank you for being such a good sport, Mr. Craig."

"I am nothing but that. Goodbye, Miss Steele, and good luck to you."

He bid the others farewell and departed from the room. He might be her last hope in Wetherfield, but she could not wish him back.

Richard took his place on the sofa and immediately she was at ease. She couldn't help whispering, "Late again, I see."

He tipped his head toward her and whispered back. "I like to keep you in suspense."

"Whatever for?"

"The more you miss me, the more I get you thinking about me."

She snorted, which made Mama turn and give her a disapproving look. She ignored Mama, keeping her tone, and whispered, "Is this part of your charm?"

"Charm? No." His teasing smile turned suddenly somber. His answer was said slowly, as if each word meant something to him. "But I would be remiss if I did not admit to enjoying seeing your eyes light up and your smile widen when I enter the room. So, if in missing me your thoughts turn to hoping, and your hopes turn to longing, then perhaps I have finally done something right in my life."

She stared at him, completely unable to speak. She had not expected him to say something so . . . so . . . romantic. But how could he torment her so when she knew that he must marry Ruth?

She glanced at Mama, whose needle wasn't moving at all. Her head was tipped to the side, as if craning her ear in their direction. She had to speak with Richard alone.

"Mama!"

Mama snapped straight in her seat. "Y-yes?"

"Would you be so good to invite Ruth to join us? I do believe she will hide if any maid comes to search for her, but she will not resist your command. And Mr. Graham dearly wants to speak to her."

Richard's brow furrowed, but she ignored him and stared pointedly at Mama.

Mama seemed confused by the directions, but that was exactly what Grace was hoping for. She set down her sewing and stood. "I shall only be a moment."

"Thank you, Mama."

As soon as she quitted the room, Grace turned to Richard. "We only have a few minutes, so we must speak quickly."

"Ah, that was clever of you. I thought you were going to hasten my proposal."

She latched on to the hesitancy in his voice, trying to read through his words. "Not just yet. There is something I must understand first. Do you *want* to marry Ruth?"

He opened and closed his mouth twice before he answered. "I didn't tell you everything about my Aunt Edith's generous offer. She listed specific qualifications for my bride."

Grace set her jaw. "Such as?"

"Lives in Wetherfield, musical, reserved, a great reader of philosophy, only passably pretty." His words slowed as he said that last part, his eyes passing over each of her features.

Did he think her passably pretty? She threw the thought from her head, knowing it did not matter. Had she not heard what he had said? She had to confirm the rest. "That night at the ball. Your riddle was about this, wasn't it? And I answered Ruth."

Pain lanced across his face and he dipped a nod. "Yes, it was why Ruth became the object of my attention."

Grace crushed the sides of her gown beneath her fingertips, not knowing if she should be angry, devastated, or both. "And without Ruth, you lose Belside?" Beautiful Belside. Her second home.

He nodded again, this time with great reluctance. "There is no excuse for any of this. But if it helps, I have been relentless in my efforts to discover a better solution. My aunt is eccentric and determined. Not to mention, the impossibility of arguing with a dying woman, but her offer is greater than any I could discover. There is one venture my solicitor stumbled upon, but I could lose everything. He has advised us to retrench for the next decade and let the house. My mother . . ."

"Your mother would not survive it," she finished for him. "Not mentally, at least."

He sighed. "Perhaps not. You know as well as I that she has not recovered from losing Father. I hope her trip to Bath is helping, but I do not expect it to heal her completely so soon. If she leaves Belside, it needs to be her choice, and not out of necessity." He shook his head. "You must know that I was determined to love Ruth—to do my best by her. Gracie, I did not expect for you and I . . ." His voice trailed off.

He picked up her hands and rubbed his thumbs over the backs of her palms, leaving a trail of heat that she felt all the way to her chest.

"I understand," she said quickly, fighting the pricking of emotion in her throat. "You're making the right decision."

"Am I?" He clung tighter to her hands.

She forced herself to nod. "You're putting your family and your future as your priority."

The skin around his eyes pulled tight. "Indeed, my sister's and my mother's happiness were the only part that kept me from walking away altogether. I thought my aunt's will was a blessing I had prayed into existence, but now I feel quite ungrateful. I want much more than a mere house for my future. I want a woman who challenges me to be better and makes the hard bearable with one smile. Gracie, I want—"

She cut him off before he could say anything more, knowing it would be too much for her to resist. "You're running out of time, Richard." She shook her head. "There are ten days left. That is not nearly enough time to plan a wedding as it is. You have to propose to Ruth straightaway."

He stared at her like she had suddenly become a stranger to him. He dropped her hands like two hot coals and sat back.

If he couldn't figure out how to ask Ruth, then she would help him. "Bring your sister and aunt to dinner tonight. Let her meet Ruth and see you two together. We can still make this work."

"Gracie—"

The way he said her name caused an ache inside her, but she quickly cut him off. "No, Richard. You cannot change this. Remember our near scandal? We could have prematurely killed her with the shock we gave her. Your aunt despises me now, and I cannot blame her. But she will adore Ruth. Think of your family and your home. Our hearts will sort themselves with time." The lie burned on her tongue. She knew her own heart would never be the same. And by the pain behind his eyes, she knew she had wounded him. Of all the mean, flippant things she had said over the years, nothing had affected him as this.

Ruth and Mama walked into the drawing room. As she pulled away from him, she whispered, "Dinner. Please say you'll come."

Chapter 23

RICHARD SHUT HIMSELF IN his bedchamber the moment he returned to Belside. He unlocked his desk drawer and dug out the letter hidden inside. Out of the corner of his eye, his letter from his mother laid on the desk already, still unanswered. The precarious future of his home had left him with too much guilt to know how to respond. Ignoring it, he read through his aunt's stipulations again, searching for a turn of phrase or wording that he could bend to allow him the freedom to marry Grace instead.

Despite his hopes, there was nothing there to save him.

She did not meet his aunt's qualifications, but she certainly met his.

If only that was enough.

He dropped the letter and slumped into his chair. He had wanted Grace to give him permission to give up on Belside, to retrench, and to marry *her*. No, he hadn't just wanted it—he had expected it. Grace wasn't like all the other debutantes. She was resilient, brave, bold. She could thrive no matter her circumstances. He truly believed that.

But she was also loyal, and she loved his sister and mother as much as he did. He also wanted to be an honorable man and keep his responsibilities. Grace would never let him be anything less.

But had Grace accurately read his feelings in his eyes? He wanted to speak them out loud, but if he could not have her, it was better for her not to hear them. It wouldn't be fair to Ruth. Whomever he married he would devote himself to. His father might have been terrible with money, but he had at least taught him the importance of being a faithful husband.

The door opened suddenly, and only then did he realize he had not locked it. When Bridget entered, he hurriedly stuffed both the letters back into the drawer.

Her brow knit at the center. "What is that you're reading?"

"Nothing."

"It is not nothing or you wouldn't be so flustered." Her mouth pulled into a grin. "Is it a love letter?"

She wasn't going to let this go, and the last thing he needed was for her to start teasing him about Grace. It would hurt too much. "It's from Mother." He pulled out her letter and handed it to Bridget to read. There was nothing in there that she couldn't know about.

Bridget studied the letter for much too long. He thought Mother had written to her as well, but perhaps not. He hadn't thought to ask.

"Oh, Richard, why did you not tell me sooner?"

"Forgive me. I did not think to. It's a relief to know that she is improving."

"Improving? Richard, she has stomach cancer! She's dying and promising to give you money to save our estate. An estate that I thought was perfectly solvent."

His jaw tightened. He had given her the wrong letter. He snatched the paper back. "You were not meant to see this."

"Perhaps not, but now I cannot unsee it. How badly do you need Aunt's money? Never mind. It has to be very bad or you wouldn't look so miserable."

He groaned and folded his arms across his chest. "These are my choices: I marry and accept the money, we sell the estate, or we let the house—possibly securing it for future generations."

Bridget went to his bed and sat down hard on the blue coverlet, her empty stare full of shock.

He folded the letter again and shoved it in his drawer, hoping to never see it again. He locked it and let his head fall into his hands.

Bridget's voice was low, but it carried easily to him. "I understand now why Grace kept pushing Ruth toward you. She knew, didn't she?"

He nodded, his eyes tracing the wood grain of his desk.

"I had hoped . . . " she began. "I had hoped you and Grace . . . but no, I see that this is for the best. Mother is finally out of her room for more than an hour put together. Can you imagine what this would do to her?"

"I have imagined nothing else."

She nodded. "I'm sorry. That was unkind. Oh, Richard. For Mother's sake, we just have to keep the house."

He let his hands slip away and turned to face her. "For your sake as well."

Bridget chewed on her bottom lip and shook her head. "I came to tell you that Aunt plans to leave tomorrow morning. Do you think we could convince her to accept Grace instead of Ruth?"

"You know her impression of Grace as well as I. She talked of nothing else at breakfast, despite the many ideal qualities Grace possesses that I listed to the contrary."

Bridget sighed. "I suppose not. She is as stubborn as an ox."

"We have been invited to dine with the Steeles tonight. It would not be hard to seek an audience with Mr. Steele afterward and ask for Ruth's hand. I have the special license ready. I must be wed by Twelfth Night or we won't have a choice about the house."

"Twelfth Night. Oh, Richard. Will she say yes?"

He tapped his hand on the desk. "I visited with Ruth for a few moments this morning and our conversation was easier than ever. There is hope that she will accept, but Bridget, I am ashamed to say it, but part of me hopes she refuses."

Bridget bowed her head and clasped her hands together. He wasn't certain if she was thinking or praying but either one he supported. He couldn't go back to bearing this weight alone. It seemed to him that God had sent him someone already to shoulder his burdens with him. And that someone was Grace.

Chapter 24

THE DREADED DINNER PARTY had come. Mother had not been too keen on the idea of having guests over when she had wanted to give the servants a lighter load after all they had done for Christmas dinner. Grace felt terrible about it . . . as terrible as being seated next to Lady Edith. This was not the first time her clever ideas had landed her in trouble.

Richard sat across from her and tried to catch her eye. She gave the smallest shake of her head. If he dared wink at her, she would throw her spoon at him. Well, not really. Hopefully, she would think of something better if it indeed came to pass.

Lady Edith looked at her then and she quickly produced an innocent smile. Deep down, she dearly wanted to earn her approval and change her fate, even though she knew it was impossible.

"Do pass the scalloped potatoes," Lady Edith said to her.

"Of course." At least this she could handle. She lifted the platter, surprised to discover how hot it was. It slid from her fingers right in front of Lady Edith's plate and hit the table hard. Potatoes splattered in a foot radius around the platter. That foot included a sizable spot on Lady Edith's chest.

"Foolish girl!" Lady Edith exclaimed.

Bridget jumped up from her seat on the other side of her aunt and wiped at Aunt's plate. Thoroughly embarrassed, Grace lifted her napkin to Lady Edith's gown. "I'm so sorry."

"Enough!" she scolded Grace, taking her napkin out of her hand. "I can certainly wipe off a bit of potato without any assistance."

Mother motioned for a footman to come and clear away the rest of the disaster. Lovely, Grace had invited even more work for the servants. This day was going from bad to worse.

"Ruth," Bridget said suddenly. "My aunt loves to read. Have you read anything you've enjoyed lately that you might recommend?"

Bridget easily took the attention away from Grace, but in doing so, Ruth's glib ability to speak about authors and their sophisticated theories made Grace feel even more inferior than her sister. Grace only read adventure stories like *Gulliver's Travels* and *Robinson Crusoe* while avoiding all academic essays and most poetry.

"Miss Steele," Richard said, when there was a lull in conversation.

Grace jerked her head up, not expecting to be addressed. "Yes?"

"Why don't you share with my aunt one of your riddles or conundrums."

What was he doing? This was his chance to showcase Ruth to his aunt, not her. "I wouldn't want to bore Lady Edith."

"Nonsense," Papa chipped in. "I always enjoy your riddles. Lady Edith should hear one."

"Go ahead." Lady Edith set her fork down.

Grace set her hands in her lap. "I don't have my notebook with me, but I might be able to remember a short one." She thought for a moment before spouting a simple rhyme she'd created the previous year. "After Christmas, I mark the end. A time for festivity, where joy doth lend. A special day with cake in the new year. What am I, bringing the holiday's final cheer?"

Everyone was silent for a moment, waiting for Lady Edith to answer first.

Lady Edith proceeded to slap her hand on the table. "Twelfth Night."

Bridget lightly clapped her hands. "Well done, Aunt."

"Let's hear another one." Lady Edith was clearly used to being obeyed.

Another? Good heavens. "I know many silly ones," she said, "but I do not think you would appreciate them. I will try to think of one you might enjoy."

Richard cleared his throat. "I have one."

Grace blinked back her surprise. "Please, go ahead."

Richard met her gaze and held it. "Tucked in green leaves, hanging high above, I have the power to spark new love. What am I, that invites a sweet embrace, never to be forgotten in one special place?"

His words propelled her back several days to their moment under the mistletoe. That kiss had changed everything. Richard had not just started a spark but a flame inside her. It had built with every moment, and whether they were together or apart, her emotions threatened to consume her.

He shouldn't be looking at her this way. He shouldn't be reminding her of that intimate moment and what might have been.

"Mistletoe," Lady Edith shouted.

Richard broke their intense connection to look at his aunt. "Well done," he whispered, his voice almost hoarse.

The older woman beamed after her triumphant guess. "I never knew I was partial to riddles."

Certainly, no riddle had ever touched Grace in the same way as this one. Not once had one been delivered with such a loving gaze and a plea to be understood either. Blinking back tears, she pretended to eat, while the others attempted a few riddles of their own.

Dinner finally ended, and they gathered in the drawing room. Music took over as the source of entertainment. Ruth played marvelously. Grace sat by Bridget, but though Richard stood on the other end of the room, she could feel the heat of his stare on her.

It was no use. She didn't want him to ask for Ruth's hand. She didn't want him to be an honorable man. She squeezed her eyes shut, hating herself for her selfish thoughts.

In the middle of a piece by Handel, Richard pulled her father aside and the two of them slipped from the room. Grace's heart thudded like the drums before an execution. He would ask for Ruth's hand, and it would be over. And she had no intention of standing in his way.

As they gathered at the door to bid goodnight, Grace could not meet Richard's eye. She didn't want to see how he felt. Relieved? Guilty? Sad? Richard exited first, then Bridget. Lady Edith was last.

"Wait." She couldn't let Lady Edith leave without speaking her peace. She hurried to her side. "I thought of one last riddle for you to take with you."

Surprisingly the interruption did not bring a frown. "Oh? All right. I find I enjoy these little guessing games. Tell me what it is."

Grace was happy she had pleased her, but this riddle was not meant for entertainment. She spoke slowly, forming the right words in the moment. "Twelfth Night brings an unexpected plan concerning heart, home, and a precious land. Hands are joined, hearts are torn. I have the power to bring love or scorn. Who am I?"

Lady Edith's wrinkled brow furrowed in question.

Grace did not wait for her to respond. "Please consider what I have said. Goodnight and safe travels."

Lady Edith eyed her strangely, her voice thoughtful. "Goodnight, Miss Steele."

Chapter 25

"This morning has been a complete and utter disaster." Bridget folded her arms across her chest and glared at him from the bottom of the staircase.

He caught the faint noise of Aunt Edith's carriage rumbling out of their drive on her way to York to visit his cousin Rose. He wished her better luck than he had had. "Aunt Edith is convinced Ruth is perfect for me."

"Like I said, it's a disaster."

He agreed, but nothing he said now would comfort either of them. They had both tried to sway her to accept Grace. They had at least made progress in helping her to believe Grace was not a heathen. Dinner with her family had helped with that. He sighed. But one evening with Ruth and her music and Aunt had been smitten by her completely. Aunt's final parting had included a warning to marry Ruth or lose the money.

Bridget spun on her heel and marched up the stairs to her bedchamber. He wished to behave the same way, but it wouldn't change their situation. It had been silly to rely on Aunt anyway. No matter how hard he tried, nothing could entice him to rush to the altar with Grace's sister.

Concerns for his mother sent him to his office to review the investment proposition from his solicitor again. He pored over numbers for hours, weighing different scenarios and cost-to-benefit considerations as a single miscalculation might spell ruin for his family. Could he risk everything he had? Would Grace still have him if he failed?

As the morning turned to early afternoon, he stood to stretch his legs, making his way to the drawing room. The house felt incredibly empty and quiet. Maybe Grace would come to visit and—

He broke off the trail of his thoughts. No Grace wouldn't come. Not today. Not for a while probably. And surely not when he was home.

Bridget sat on the sofa and turned away from him as he entered the room. Was she still angry with him? She had every right to be. He was failing in every direction he looked.

Richard went straight to the fireplace and rested his forearms on the mantle, letting it bear his weight as he leaned heavily against it. Bridget sniffed behind him, pouring salt into his wounded heart. He hated it when she cried.

The room was quiet for a time. His sister, no doubt, silently cursed his failures while he ruminated over the same thing. The curling flames licked the logs beneath the hearth. It might as well have been his budding hopes and dreams for the future being burned to a crisp. He missed Grace already, and he had been parted from her for less than a day. She would know how to comfort Bridget. Her presence would comfort him too. Grinding his teeth together, he prayed for fortitude.

"I've always wanted to call Grace my sister." Bridget's words were hardly more than a whisper, but they effectively broke the silence between them and froze him in place. "I was willing to give up my position as her best friend, knowing you would stand in that prominent place after you wed—indeed, I have seen you already sliding into that role these past weeks." He listened intently to her slowly spun words, each one weighted and heavy. "She's already family to me, Richard, and she means more to me than this old house."

He pushed away from the mantel and turned to face her. "In truth?"

She lifted her eyes to meet his, wiping at her wet cheeks. "Believe me when I say, I want you to be happy. Marry whomever you choose, but you know who I would pick for you."

Sudden emotion clawed at his throat, and he tried to swallow it down. "Dare I choose the same woman who would murder me in my bed should I vex her?"

A small smile touched her mouth. "The very same."

A soft chuckle escaped. "We Grahams have good taste."

"The very best."

He clasped his hands behind his back and dropped his gaze to the blue Axminster carpet at his feet. "I appreciate having you on my side, but if it was just about you or me, I wouldn't be standing here right now. I would forget the state of our finances and be on Grace's doorstep begging for her hand. I love her, Bridget. I love her so much that if I cannot discover a solution, I might go mad." He was breathing hard. He met Bridget's wide, sorrowful eyes. "But nothing is so simple. What about your future? Your happiness wears on my conscience. And what about Mother?"

A voice cleared from the doorway. "What about your mother?"

Richard's head jerked to find his mother, standing with her arms crossed. "Mother? You're home early!"

Bridget jumped to her feet, but Mother held up a hand to stop her.

Several inches shorter than Bridget, Mother stood with her chin lifted, which made her appear somehow taller than usual. Indeed, she seemed more sure of herself than she had been since Father's death.

Her cheeks had color in them again, and her brown eyes, while still lined with fatigue, were brighter and clearer than before.

While he wanted to rejoice in her improved appearance, he was stuck on one thought. How much had she overheard? And would it send her health spiraling backward should she know the whole truth?

Mother smoothed her puce traveling gown as she entered the room, stopping at the edge of the sofa. "I wanted to be with my children for Twelfth Night. It seems my arrival is timely. What is this about the state of our finances, and when exactly did you fall in love with Grace?"

Richard's mouth dropped open. His eyes darted to Bridget's, which were equally concerned. There would be no scheming their way out of this one. "Mother, I believe you had better sit down."

"I have been sitting for hours in a carriage and prefer to stand."

"Very well." Richard began by explaining how the previous solicitor and Father had not managed the estate funds well and his failed attempts to rectify it on his own. Then he shared about Aunt's will and her stipulations for him to inherit. He left out the part about courting Grace to acquire Ruth's acceptance but finished with how he had fallen in love with Grace this past month and how Aunt was convinced against her.

Mother swayed a bit and extended a hand to steady herself on the sofa.

With several large strides, he reached her side and took her arm. Bridget placed herself on her other side.

"I am well," Mother assured. "I need a moment alone and a little tea is all."

"Of course," Richard said. "Let me take you to your bedchamber."

She shook her head. "The chaise lounge in the library will do."

He sent a worried frown over her head at Bridget, who shrugged helplessly. Flanking her side, they led Mother to the library and left her to rest with a blanket on her lap and a warm fire behind the grate. He could only hope a little refreshment would ease her shock, but such a wish seemed foolish.

What had he done? Should he have proposed to Ruth? He dug his hands in his hair the moment he was free from the library. Where were all the Christmas miracles that promised an abundance of love, happy homes, and healthy families?

Certainly not anywhere near him.

Chapter 26

GRACE NIBBLED HALF-HEARTEDLY ON her breakfast, observing her family carefully. No one acted as if anything unusual had occurred the night before over dinner. Ruth seemed especially oblivious. Where was the announcement of her engagement? The talk of weddings?

Biting into her warm bread and butter, she chewed furiously, not tasting any part of it. She swallowed down a lump and forced herself to pry out answers. "Father, did you enjoy the dinner last night?"

He lowered his newspaper and grunted. "I always enjoy dinner."

She tried again. "What about our company?"

"Pleasant."

Pleasant? That was a remark on the weather, not a person. She required specific information. "Did you and Mr. Graham discuss anything interesting?"

He folded his paper. "Our conversation is always interesting. Are you asking if your name was brought up?"

She sputtered. "My name? Certainly not. Why would you speak of me?" Her cheeks burned worse than the steaming sausage on her plate. At least she was not crying. She had done enough of that last night, hiding her sobs in her pillow.

"Because he lost his senses," Tobias answered. "What man makes riddles about mistletoe?" Her brother curled his lip in disgust.

Her father laughed and picked up his paper again.

Grace stole a glance at Ruth. Every time she looked at her, jealousy threatened to erupt in her throat. Ruth had an open book on her lap, partially hidden by the tablecloth. Their parents hadn't seen it yet, but it was obvious that Ruth was absorbed in a story and not at all aware of her future nuptials. Otherwise, she was certain Ruth would be incapable of reading.

A footman came in carrying a letter. Instead of stopping at Papa's side or walking to Mama, he stopped at Grace's side and extended the folded paper.

"For me?"

He nodded.

Was it from Richard? She accepted the letter and turned it over to see the address. It was from her aunt in London.

Ripping into it, she read the contents and sighed with relief. She could leave this place. It was the only way to breathe fully again.

"Who is it from?" Mama asked.

"My aunt in London is requesting again that I come for the Season. She is promising new gowns and invitations to popular assemblies. Please, Mama, won't you consider it?"

Mama sighed and looked at Papa. "I am leaving this argument up to you, dearest."

"Should I thank you?" Papa asked, grimacing. "Grace, my sweet, we will discuss it after the holidays."

Could she make it that long in this small town? She was bound to run into Richard, and if that did not kill her, discussing wedding details with Ruth would.

"How about after the new year? Can we discuss it then?"

Papa tightened his hold on his paper. "Very well, we can have a short conversation about it then."

Hallelujah. There was hope!

"But don't get your hopes up," Papa added, likely reading the expression on her face. "I have a feeling that this spring will be eventful, and you will want to be here for it."

She blinked several times. Eventful? Like a wedding?

"I don't care for events," she said, pushing at the crumbs on her plate with her fork.

Papa chuckled as if he knew something she did not. He looked up and winked at Mama. Mama only shook her head, but a small smile touched her lips.

What was that about?

She had eternity to wonder about it.

And in her wondering, she had to resist racing over to Belside to discuss it with Bridget. One look at Richard and she would beg him to give up everything so they could be together.

No, she would have to suffer alone until her parents let her leave for London. She angrily shoved a large bite of toast into her mouth.

"That reminds me," Mama said. "Bridget left one of her gloves in the entrance hall. Be a good girl and return it to her?"

"What?" Bread crumbs spewed over her gown and plate. She brushed herself off with a napkin. "I am terribly busy today. Ruth could take it."

"I cannot," Ruth said, jerking her gaze away from her book. It was a wonder how she could listen and read at the same time. "I have been invited to a musical club with Miss Craig."

"Miss Craig?" Since when were they friends? She couldn't even invite herself along for multiple reasons. Drat.

"Tobias?"

He stood, wiping his mouth with the back of his hand. "I am practicing my fencing. Mr. Graham promised to spar with me soon. I need to practice."

Of course he did. That man was entirely too entangled into her life.

"Couldn't you take it, Mama?" At this rate, she might be forced to run away without their permission. She couldn't go to Belside. She wouldn't!

"Nonsense, I am delivering charity baskets with the vicar's wife today. And don't ask your father. He hasn't the time. You, on the other hand, have nothing pressing today."

Grace batted her hand. "Certainly there is no rush for a mere glove. She has spares."

"I wouldn't be so sure. She grew a whole two inches this last year, and her mother has not been well enough to see to all the changes in her wardrobe. I will feel personally responsible if she is invited to dinner somewhere and must refuse because of something so easily remedied."

But who would invite them to dinner? Bridget did not dine out often. She closed her eyes and squeezed them tightly. But if she was invited, she deserved to go out. She of all people needed outings and more opportunities to meet people.

Dear, merciful heavens. She was going to have to go to Belside.

Chapter 27

RICHARD COULD NOT REMEMBER the last family council the Grahams had had, but there was no better description for this particular meeting. He and Bridget had pulled chairs beside the slate-colored chaise Mother had not moved from after she had requested a maid fetch them.

She was sitting straight and her pallor had significantly improved from when they had helped her to rest not a half hour previously.

"I'm sorry you had to return to bad news," he said, bracing his hands together.

Her lips quivered. "If anyone should apologize it is me. I should never have let my grief carry away all my good sense while you two were left to mourn without my comfort. Now you look at me as if a disappointment—albeit a large one—will be the death of me."

"Oh, Mother," Bridget said, reaching for her hand. "You have suffered so much. Of course, we worry."

Mother accepted the hand, but shook her head. "Richard might be the patriarch of this family now, but he still needs a mother, just as you do, Bridget. No burden as great as this should be born alone."

He agreed, but he was a capable adult, and while he was alive, his mother should not be made to bear any more than she already had. "It is good to have you home again. That is comfort enough. Please, do not worry overmuch about the house. I will find a way to save it."

"We will find a way together," Mother corrected, reaching to take his hand too. "I am stronger now. Indeed, I feel strong enough to climb back into a carriage to meet with your solicitor."

"What?" Bridget drew back while Richard leaned forward in his seat.

"Why would you need to meet with my solicitor?" he asked.

She shrugged. "We have a great deal to discuss."

His brow rose. "Discuss what, exactly?" He wasn't certain his mother was thinking straight. Surely, she was overtired.

"Discuss your wedding to Grace. Bridget, fetch your writing things and a paper. I have a letter to write before we depart."

Bridget gave him a wild look of hope, excitement, and fear all wrapped together before catapulting to her feet and rushing out the door in a very unladylike fashion.

It appeared Richard would have to be the one to speak reason to Mother. "I am not certain you understand the situation, Mother."

"I understand perfectly. Grace convinced me to leave my bed, and she has kept Bridget from succumbing to her sorrows, and it seems she has mended your heart as well. As far as I am concerned, Grace has saved this family. She belongs to us now. I am content to retrench and say goodbye to Belside." She took in the room, her eyes tracing the walls and furniture, and her lip quivered again. "It holds memories but not our happiness. That is something we find anywhere so long as we are together."

He couldn't believe what he was hearing. He climbed from his chair and kneeled down beside her. "Are you certain?"

She gave a firm nod. "I cannot encourage an investment scheme that might put us worse off than we already are. This makes the most sense. Ruth is a good girl, a very good girl, but she is not your other half. None of us would be happy here if you weren't. But with Grace, we all have a fighting chance."

He bent his head so his forehead rested on the edge of his mother's lap, relief filling every inch of him. That she and his sister would sacrifice so much for him trapped his words in his throat.

Mother ran her hand through his hair. "We can go over the details on our way. I want to find a cottage that will comfortably fit us all, and these matters take time to get right."

He lifted his head and stared at his mother. Moisture glazed her eyes. "Can we really do this?"

She captured his hands in her much smaller ones. "We can and we will. While I was in Bath, I spent an afternoon walking along the park outside of the Royal Crescent. I stood back to admire the beauty when I felt your father say in my mind, 'The world holds far more beautiful sights, but none is greater than witnessing the joy of your children.' Regret filled me with all the precious time I had lost during my mourning. A few changes are in order, so I won't succumb to sorrows again. For starters, I won't be returning to my room again, Richard. I want a guest room prepared for me. I cannot promise I won't cry occasionally, but I am determined to live in the present."

He squeezed her hands. "If that is what you wish."

"It is." She set her hand on his shoulders and pulled him to her. Her hug was the balm he needed. Her renewed strength was tangible hope he could grasp onto.

Bridget returned with her writing things, and Mother quickly penned a letter to his aunt. "I want her to know exactly what I think about this confounded situation. I'll address it to your cousin so she receives it before she leaves York."

His mother's boldness made them laugh.

"She will not like you interfering," he cautioned.

"She interfered first, did she not?"

Richard and Bridget shared an amused look. Grace had been very wise to encourage Mother to leave. She had returned with her old spirit back.

"Just remember, she is a very sick woman, and please be kind," he begged.

"We all love Aunt Edith," Mother said. "But sick or not, I cannot be easy until I share with her my feelings."

He had on his greatcoat and the women their cloaks, and they were nearly to the front door when someone knocked on the other side.

"Who could that be?" Bridget asked.

Not bothering to wait for a footman or his butler to answer it, he opened it himself. "Grace?"

She stared wide-eyed at him from beneath her bonnet. "I . . . uh . . . Bridget forgot her glove."

She extended her hand to him with the glove inside it.

He grinned, so incredibly happy to see her, even if she hadn't come for him. Maybe it was her canary-yellow pelisse, but she was as radiant as the sun. "Why do you not give it to her yourself?" He clasped his hand around her extended one and pulled her toward him.

She stumbled forward, which gave him the excuse to put his arm around her back too. She went as rigid as a fence post. A cold fence post in need of warming, and he was all too happy to volunteer.

Once she was through the door, she gasped. "Mrs. Graham, you're home!"

Mrs. Graham grinned like Richard hadn't seen her grin since before Father's death.

"Dearest Grace. My dear, dear, girl. How happy I am to see you."

Richard reluctantly released Grace long enough for his mother to take a turn embracing her.

"Your cheeks are rosy again," Grace said, her own smile appearing. "You returned to us with the spritely look that would put the young debutantes to shame."

Mother cupped her hand around Grace's chin. "Your flattery is full of shameful lies, but I won't make you take them back."

They all laughed—Richard's more of wonder than humor.

"What is it you said about a glove?" Bridget asked.

"Oh, yes. You forgot yours last night." Grace held out the glove to Bridget.

Bridget accepted it and held it up. "But this is not mine."

"Is it not?" Grace frowned. "My mother was certain it was yours."

"Odd," Bridget fingered the lace on the end. "Does not your mother have a pair like this?"

Grace snatched it back and examined it closer. "That deceitful woman! I was distracted and did not look at it properly."

Mother laughed. "You mean, wise woman. Bridget and I will wait in the carriage. I think you two have a few things to say to each other."

Grace's gaze flew to his, and her eyes welled with panic.

"You are absolutely right, Mother. We do have a few things to speak about."

Mother and Bridget shared a conspiratorial look and linked arms, waltzing from the house.

"Take all the time you need," Bridget giggled, blowing them both a kiss. She never was one for subtlety.

They shut the door behind them. There was not a better time for Mother to forget all those lessons on propriety. His grin hadn't left him, and he sauntered toward Grace. Finally, he could speak his heart.

Chapter 28

"WHAT ARE YOU DOING?" Grace took a panicked step backward, then another. Had her mother knowingly sent her into this trap?

"We're having a talk," he said. Why was he smiling like that? Why was he smiling at all? Shouldn't he be as upset as she was?

She furiously shook her head. "But you aren't saying anything."

"Not all communication requires talking, but there are a few words that need to be said. Gracie May Steele, I'm in love with you."

Her breath caught. Love? Her? "W-what about Ruth?"

"I made it much more complex than I needed it to be, but the answer is rather simple. I choose you."

Her laugh came out high-pitched and strained. "You're teasing me again." Her next step backward was matched with his step forward. It couldn't be true, no matter how hard she had wished it. Could she be dreaming?

"I haven't been teasing for a long time." He pointedly glanced up, and her eyes followed his gaze. Somehow, they had ended up under the infamous mistletoe . . . again.

"You wouldn't dare," she whispered, her own smile erupting.

He leaned toward her. "I've heard that before. Right before I was called a coward."

Her heart beat an anticipatory staccato in her chest. "That couldn't have been me."

He reached up and pulled one of her bonnet strings, releasing it from its bow. "Who else?"

She cleared her throat. "I don't think you're a coward." She might be, but he was definitely not.

"You're just trying to get out of this kiss. But I wouldn't be a gentleman if I passed up a *tradition.*"

Good heavens. "You remember that, do you?"

He nodded long and slow. "I remember everything you say."

She bit her bottom lip as if hiding it from him, completely unprepared. "All of it?"

"Every precious word."

He'd barely finished his sentence before his head lowered and there was no more hiding her lips from him, nor did she want to. He loved her. He had chosen her. Her bonnet dropped to the floor, while her spirits soared. Last time had been a surprise, like two hearts accidentally bumping into each other, sparks igniting. This time was different. Their two hearts had grown close, and each movement of their mouths stoked the flames between them until they grew into a full-fledged fire.

Her hands could not hold him close enough. She wanted forever with him. He reciprocated, holding her firmly against him, his touch cherishing and passionate.

Richard pulled back long enough to whisper, "Now you will be my home," before his lips found hers again.

The shock of his words made her push him back again. "But Richard. What about Belside?"

His lips finally relinquished their furtive intentions, his heady gaze sobering. "Do you mind so very much being poor?"

She gave a short laugh of amazement. "How could I if I was rich in my heart?"

"Do you love me then, Gracie?"

"I think I've always loved you, Richard. I've just been fighting the feeling for a very long time."

His smile reemerged. "There's plenty else to fight about, so let's stop fighting this."

"Richard, I—"

He put his finger to her lips, as if sensing her argument. "I don't have all the answers yet. I have some business to work out first. Will you wait for me? I am not certain how long it will take us to sort everything."

She thought of her aunt's letter inviting her to London but immediately tossed the idea aside. "Of course, I will wait."

He kissed her again, this time a short peck that was not nearly long enough. "I will come to see you as soon as we return."

She nodded, reluctantly releasing him. Happiness swirled with guilt. In accepting his love, she was ruining so much for him and his family. Were they making the right choice?

He swiped her bonnet from the floor and set it back on her head, smoothing the hair by her cheeks that had no doubt become loosened during his kisses. His hand slid to her ribbons, and she watched amazed as he tied it for her. His gentle, featherlike touch on her neck sent gooseflesh down the whole of her.

When he met her gaze again, he winked and stepped back. "Don't forget to miss me. You know how I appreciate it when you long for my return."

Laughing, she gave him a playful shove. "Hurry so I do not have to pine overlong."

He dipped his head and left her alone in the entrance hall of Belside. She should have left at the same time, but this manor had become so much like her own that she had forgotten it was not her home too.

Turning in a circle, she studied the thick white trim edged with gold paint, the columns by the door, the pale painted walls, the gleaming crystal chandelier. She had been weak just now, letting Richard give all of this up.

Sighing, she relented to leave the decision with him. Meeting with his solicitor could jolt him back to the harsh reality of his situation, but she had promised to wait for him, and she would.

Chapter 29

Of all the virtues her parents could have named her, it was wise of them not to have christened her Patience. Waiting for Richard was impossibly hard. Her ears strained for the sound of carriage wheels on the drive, every bump of noise resembling a knock on the front door and every minute passing slower than the previous one.

Three long days away from Richard were enough to drive a woman mad.

What was happening? Had he changed his mind? It was the new year, and there were still a few days left until Twelfth Night . . . still time for him and Ruth to marry. As for her, she would go to London and cry the whole time, only to return to marry Mr. Dobson.

"Grace, you do not look well at all," Ruth said, finding her by the window in the drawing room.

Grace leaned against the cold glass where she had the best view of the road. "I'm not quite myself, but I am well enough."

"We haven't seen Mr. Graham or Bridget for a few days now, and you have not left the house to visit them. Is everything all right between you?"

Mother had asked the same thing that very morning. Grace had thought Richard had asked Papa for Ruth's hand at their last dinner together, but no one seemed to think anything of that sort. Indeed, they dropped hints that they assumed he would ask for Grace's any day now. She couldn't bring herself to respond to their insinuations.

"They have left town."

Ruth's brow rose and she tilted her chin. "You never said anything. Where did they go and for how long?"

She did not think it her place to explain about Graham's finances. Whether Richard proposed marriage to Ruth or not, their secret would not stay covered for long. But the details would not be gossiped about from her. "I cannot say exactly. I thought they would be back by now."

Ruth squeezed in on the window ledge beside her. "Did they go to Bath to fetch Mrs. Graham?"

"No, Mrs. Graham returned just before they left."

Ruth smiled. "Do you not think it's strange how ingrained you are into their family?"

Grace shook her head. "Of course not. I love them. And it is only natural for a person to know about the ones they care for."

"You love all of them? But especially Mr. Graham?"

She met Ruth's knowing gaze and could not look away.

Ruth grinned. "I have been waiting years for you to admit it."

"Years?" She repeated, unable to deny what her sister had seen.

Ruth nodded. "There is not a man's name you have spoken more than his. I think it's wonderful too. I, myself, will never settle for less than love."

"Truly?" Grace asked, unsure if she should say what was on her mind. "Then . . . then you could never marry Mr. Graham if, say, he proposed to you?"

Ruth scoffed. "Never in a million years. I had started to believe all the insults you paid to his name, but I can honestly say that I find him tolerable enough to be called my brother someday. Getting to know him this past month has strengthened my opinion of him. However, I could never care for him in the way you do." She frowned. "Why would you ask that?"

Grace sighed and ducked her head. "His aunt thinks you are perfect for him."

Ruth gave her a pointed stare. "What a foolish notion to keep in your head. What matters is what Mr. Graham thinks, and it is obvious that he adores you."

"What if . . . what if I did not agree with what he wanted to sacrifice in order to be together?"

Ruth shrugged. "I cannot answer well without knowing more details, but would it not be his sacrifice to make and not yours?"

"Yes, but it affects more than him."

"I see. If his heart is in the right place, you must trust that it will all work out. Or . . ."

"Or?" she held her breath.

"You can turn him down."

Ruth might as well have sunk a knife into her chest. "Thank you for your advice."

Ruth patted her lap. "What are older sisters for?"

The sound of gravel crunching through the window pierced her ears and kept her from responding. She whirled around, hands flying to the glass. The Grahams' carriage!

"He's here." She stepped away from the window, smoothing her dress and then her hair. "He's really here."

"Stop fussing and breathe a little," Ruth laughed.

"Breathe? How can I breathe?" Her lungs tightened and her heart pounded against her ribs. She shook her hands in the air, trying to shake off the mounting anxiety. "How do I look? Should I run upstairs and put on some rouge? Or a necklace? I should have worn a necklace today."

Ruth shook her head. "I have never seen you like this."

"I should hope not. I have never felt this maddening suffocation before."

"So that's what love feels like? Perhaps I can wait a little longer for my turn." Ruth turned to peer through the window. "Here he comes."

She squeezed her hands together. "Is he with his family?"

Ruth grinned. "He's alone." She swept past Grace. "I will see that you are too."

"Wait, don't leave me!" Grace cried.

Ruth only laughed and skirted away.

Time, now conscious of its ill behavior the last few days, did the opposite and sped forward. She hadn't time to collect herself. Taking several deep breaths, she repeated in her mind Ruth's advice. *Trust that it will all work out.*

Surprisingly, it helped, and when Richard came into the drawing room and bowed to her, she was as ready as she would ever be to hear the outcome of his trip.

He lifted his head and smiled.

It wasn't wide, or teasing, sad, or forced. What did it mean?

"H-how was your trip?"

"We secured a cottage about an hour's drive from here. It's significantly smaller than Belside, but there are rooms enough, sufficient funds for a few servants, and enough land for a garden and chickens. Mr. Bowers believes he might have a generous renter. It is not ideal, but our children will inherit a good life."

Had she heard him right? "Our children?"

He nodded, coming toward her with steady, confident steps. "You know, the ones you and I create together."

She slapped his shoulder when he reached her. "You cannot say such things!"

"I like when you fight me, but I prefer the passion of your kisses." He wrapped his arms around her, and she fell against him.

"Shh! Someone will hear you." She expected her mother to rush in at any moment to find them entangled together.

"I hope they do. I plan to marry you, Gracie Steele."

Her argument died on her lips. "You want to marry me?" Her very soul seemed to light up inside her, bursting with joy.

He stroked the skin along her collarbone. "It isn't London, but who else would ensure I stay humble all my days?"

"Hang London," she said. "I am the only one you can trust to care for your ego."

"Only you." He kissed her nose. "Then only you for me."

She rested her hands on his rising chest. "I don't want you to regret choosing me. My dowry is small and will not go far. This opportunity with your aunt will never come again."

He smoothed the wisps of hair at her temples. "How could I regret this beautiful woman in my arms? I have been counting down the minutes until I could hold you again."

"You've been thinking about me?" She stared at him in awe. This sought-after man, adored by every woman in the world, had missed her? She could not get used to it.

He dropped another kiss on her mouth. "Constantly."

See reason, she told herself. Reason! "But your mother . . ."

The surety in his eyes spoke before he did. "She knows and supports us."

Even if that were true, could her health sustain her support? "And your sister? Will Bridget still have a dowry?"

He paused. "Likely not."

She shook her head. "Richard, it's too much."

"No house with all its splendor and finery could be enjoyable without you in it. Bridget has relinquished her dowry for the honor of having you as a sister. And mother? Her tears over the land have been exchanged for tears of happiness over anticipating having such a prize for a daughter-in-law."

She could barely hold back the emotion brimming inside her. "And you?"

He seemed to breathe her in. "If my home collapses with not a brick left in place, I will still rejoice if it means you are by my side."

The happiest of tears teetered over the edge when her cheeks lifted into a small smile. "You're too wonderful, Richard Graham."

He wiped at the moisture spilling down her cheeks with the pad of his thumb. "Is that a yes?"

Lifting up on her toes, she placed a chaste kiss on his mouth. "A resounding yes."

Chapter 30

BEFORE CALLING HOURS OFFICIALLY began, Richard stopped by Callis Hall with his family's old sleigh. With a little sharpening and grease, it would last another few winters, but without the proper storage at their new cottage, it was on the list of items to remain behind at Belside. Even though there was hardly enough snow to warrant using it, he had been unable to resist one last ride. He patted the trusty conveyance before striding inside the house, ready to meet with Grace's father and request his permission for her hand in marriage.

Mr. Steele met him at his office door and invited him inside. The familiar room eased Richard's mounting nerves. The night his aunt had come to dine at Callis Hall with him he had previously relayed to Mr. Steele specific details of his financial situation, many of which Mr. Steele had guessed at.

Once they sat down, he added the tale of his aunt's will, his rejection of it in favor of marrying Grace, and the cottage he had secured for his family.

"I know it is not the ideal setting to marry," Richard hedged, "but I hope the friendship between our families will carry some weight in your decision. Indeed, I will endeavor to do all I can to see Grace is given every comfort."

Mr. Steele clasped his hands on his desk and leaned forward in his seat. "I trust you will. This past year or more, you have proven yourself to be a responsible man. If you had come to me with the details of your aunt's will and asked for Ruth's hand, I would have said no. Money is important, but your choice to sacrifice it for my daughter's happiness shows true character. Granted, I fully expect you to work hard at returning to Belside as quickly as possible."

"Yes, sir."

When he left Mr. Steele's office, he heaved a sigh. Grace appeared in the corridor like an apparition inspired by his desire to see her. She wore her cloak and mittens and an excited smile.

"Are you going somewhere?" he asked.

"On a sleigh ride with you, of course."

He laughed and extended his hand. "Then by all means, let's be on our way."

Once they were bundled beneath a heavy wool blanket inside the sleigh, and being pulled just beyond Callis Hall's drive, he was ready to answer the set of questioning eyes next to him.

"Yes, I met with your father to ask for your hand."

She feigned innocence. "Oh? Is that what you were doing? And did he happen to give you an answer?"

"He did."

"And?"

He shrugged.

A swift elbow met his ribs. He chuckled, putting both the reins in one hand so he could put his other around her. "He gave his permission."

She squealed and kissed his cheek.

"It will take time to get settled at the cottage, find tenants for Belside, and make certain our finances are stable." He hesitated before he said the hardest part. "It could be a year or more before we can wed."

She did not say anything, and a quick glance did not reveal her feelings. The horses were already walking at a slow pace, but he pulled them to a stop and turned to her.

"What do you think?" he asked. "I want your complete honesty." As for him, after the ache of not knowing if they could be together, it felt like a lifetime to wait any longer. He caught a glimpse of the same longing, but she hid it behind a smile.

Grace set her hand on his arm. "Let's wed one year from now, on Twelfth Night."

There was energy in her statement—excitement—and it relieved his worries.

"Why not? All month the idea of Twelfth Night and weddings have been tied together in my mind. The only part missing was the image of you by my side."

She leaned into his shoulder and he tucked the fur blanket more securely around her. "I might be by your side forever now, but don't let my complete devotion go to your head."

He set the horses to walking again. "It's too late. My hat is already feeling tight from the swelling."

She nudged him. "It is a good thing I love more than just your appearance."

"Indeed? Then what is it about me that finally won you over?"

"Your kiss."

"Is that all?" he laughed.

"Your aunt was not all wrong. Holidays are romantic. A mistletoe kiss can be very convincing."

"Are you suggesting that your regard for me is entirely unrelated to my own merits?"

One brow lifted. "Kissing is an important quality. Had I not learned of your skill, you might not have succeeded in winning my heart."

"I suppose I will have to keep doing so to remind you to care for me."

"You had better get started. This path is too short to waste any more time."

Eager to please her, he bent forward and kissed her cold lips. And then he had to do so again, for a gentleman could not let a lady freeze.

By the time they returned home, they discovered his mother and sister had come to visit Callis Hall in the carriage. It was good to see Mother paying calls on friends, and it was the perfect opportunity to share their plan with everyone.

"We're getting married," he said, lifting Grace's hand in the air with a flourish.

Cheers erupted and they were hugged at least twice by everyone, though Tobias settled for a single handshake. The news of their move came afterward, which invoked a few tears from Mrs. Steele, but their families rallied around them and accepted their proposed wedding date.

"We will have plenty of time to find the right wedding clothes," Mrs. Steele told his mother.

Tobias grimaced. "Of all the reasons to be excited about a wedding date. By that time, you can have a suit of clothes fitted to the horse."

Tobias's comments were ignored in the enthusiastic discussion of a wedding breakfast menu that came next.

Amused, Richard watched more than participated. Seeing their families together—his and Grace's mothers chattering excitedly side-by-side, his sister and Ruth teasing Tobias about how it would be his turn soon enough, and Mr. Steele nodding proudly at him from his relaxed position in the chair by the fire—filled him with inexpressible joy. He'd never felt closer to them than he did at this moment. There was something about coming together during times of trials and blessings that bonded family as nothing else could.

"I nearly forgot," Mother said, retrieving something from her reticule. "I received a reply from Aunt Edith today."

"What did it say?" he asked.

Mother winced. "I was too afraid to open it. Despite how you cautioned me, I might have been a tad too direct in my correspondence to her. I greatly fear I upset a sick woman."

Richard took the letter and broke the seal, bracing himself for the contents. Disappointing his aunt was not something he wanted to do at any time in his life. He cared for her opinion of him, and he believed she offered him money because she cared deeply for him too. His eyes scanned the words. "She writes that her health has not worsened with her travels."

"Thank goodness," Bridget breathed.

He read on, his eyes widening. He tapped the letter, not once but thrice. "You will not believe this!" he cried.

"What is it?" Grace leaned toward him.

He lowered the paper for her to see. "She has agreed to give me half the inheritance money if I disregard the stipulations for the bride but still manage to marry by Twelfth Night."

Amazement filled Grace's eyes. "Then we can marry sooner?"

He grinned. "Indeed, if you desire it."

Her eyes sparkled. "I do." She squeezed his arm; though he would have preferred a kiss, it was far more appropriate with their current company. "Does this mean Bridget will have a dowry again too?"

"Yes." His gaze lifted to his sister. "Bridget can have a dowry."

Bridget smiled at them. "I was never worried. I trust the two of you will see right by me."

"We will, I promise," he said.

"This is very good of your aunt," Mother said, before turning to Mrs. Steele. "She is famously stubborn."

He read further. "She writes that her family disapproved of her lowering herself to marry a merchant for love, albeit a wealthy one, and she did not want to repeat history. She said that the last riddle Grace left her, combined with your letter, Mother, and her long-standing love for Belside, convinced her to alter her decision."

"Riddle?" Ruth asked. "What riddle could that be?"

Tobias snorted. "Not the one about the mistletoe."

"Mistletoe? I would like to hear that one," Mother said.

Mrs. Steele chuckled. "Your son is a poet."

"My Richard?" she asked.

For heaven's sake. Had he really delivered that riddle over the dinner table while making moon-eyes at Grace? He smiled sheepishly. "She said specifically it was Grace's riddle, not mine."

Grace shrank under all the eyes that immediately turned her way. "I might have delivered her a few lines that implied she was toying with hearts."

He reached over and stole her hand. "A brave feat that paid off rather nicely for us all."

"I should say. She clearly dislikes me." Grace shook her head. "But after this letter, my opinion of her is altering. She is undoubtedly a most generous woman."

"A wise choice, Grace," Mr. Steele chipped in. "With the added money and your dowry, Mr. Graham will have room to invest and pay off his creditors all the sooner. You'll be back at Belside in no time."

Mrs. Steele frowned. "But Twelfth Night is in three days. What about wedding clothes?"

No one said anything for a moment.

"I think we can manage, can we not Mrs. Steele?" Mr. Steele asked. "After all, Mr. Graham will be happy to marry Grace no matter what she wears to her wedding."

"I suppose," Mrs. Steele said, "but it will not be easy to overlook it."

It was quiet again for a moment until Bridget announced, "We should have some of Aunt Edith's famous shortbread to celebrate."

Ruth nodded her agreement. "And some of Gracie's famous hot chocolate."

"Gracie's hot chocolate?" Mrs. Steele asked. "What sort of concoction is this?"

Grace laughed. "I stole the recipe from cook and altered it slightly to my taste."

Richard squeezed her hand. "I have a hankering for it myself. Let's go tell your cook ourselves about the alterations." He subtly winked at her, hoping she would catch on.

"What a splendid idea," she said, letting him help her to her feet.

Once they were in the corridor, she leaned close. "Cook already knows my recipe."

"I had to get you alone somehow."

"You charmer."

He ducked around a corner, pulling her with him. Sweeping his arms around Grace's middle, he gently placed her against the wall and out of sight.

"Are we hiding from someone?" she asked, her alluring giggle nearly undoing him.

"Everyone. It might be until after the wedding before we are alone again, and I wanted to celebrate Aunt's news properly. I was afraid

God wouldn't bless me because I had been self-absorbed for too long. Now I am at a loss for words."

"Let me guess. You celebrate by kissing?"

He chuckled, resting his forehead against hers. "I don't care what we do, so long as we are together."

"You know I don't need the walls of Belside to wake up to every morning. Your smile will be enough for me."

He smoothed her hair back in slow, smooth strokes. "There will be no removing Society's judgements when we return, but in time, we will build a strong future for our posterity. I promise you."

She slid her hands around his waist. "I trust you, Richard. No one can believe you are self-absorbed, not after all you have given up. From now on, the only time I will list your horrible qualities is to chase away unwanted company."

He put a hand to his heart. "You would do that for me?"

She reeled him back to her. "You're not the only one who likes to be alone together."

He laughed and pressed a kiss to her mouth. When he released her, he said, "I came up with another riddle for your collection."

Her eyes were heady and her smile encouraging. "Go ahead, let's hear it."

He cleared his throat and recited the words that had kept him up late into the night, hoping not to forget a single word:

At Belside manor, a maiden fair,
Frowned at a lad with light-brown hair.
He puffed his chest, strutted with pride,
And teased the girl, who cast him aside.
When death's sorrow stripped him bare,
The pretty maiden, in kindness rare,
Softened his heart, and dispelled his gloom,

Staying by his side, until joy did bloom.
As in stories of old with a twist,
She became the friend he liked to kiss.
Love emerged, and his heart's embrace,
Became his wife, his darling Grace.

Her eyes glistened with tears. "That isn't a riddle. It's poetry. The best poetry I have ever heard."

"I am an amateur, and you well know it."

"I am always honest with you, Richard, and it was perfection itself."

"It's clear you're the inspiration behind every word. You hold my happiness. I thought I had lost it after Father's death, but you brought it back to me with your witty insults, charming smiles, and loving heart. Have I told you how much I love you, Gracie?"

"Not today," Grace replied, her hand finding the hair at the back of his neck and running her fingers through it. "But I have been negligent too. You also hold my happiness. I tried to thwart the feeling for many years, but my soul knew its match even before I did. No one has ever cared for me like you do. I love you with my whole heart, Richie Graham."

Such a statement deserved rewarding. He pressed her into the wall and kissed her soundly.

Epilogue

Four Years Later

GRACE'S HALF BOOTS CRUNCHED against the thin layer of snow lining the drive. Tilting back her head, she admired the cream-colored stucco smoothing the brick surface of her new home. The tall windows gleamed, beckoning for her to look inside each and every one. Her eyes traced the iron balcony above the columned entrance to the familiar black door she had dreamed of entering again since that eventful holiday four years ago when they had been forced to leave.

"Mama, I'm cold. Can we go inside?"

Grace squeezed the small hand she held and smiled at Oliver. "Father gets to go first." She pulled his cap more snugly over his dark hair, admiring how much her growing three-year-old took after her husband. He was already a precocious, handsome little man. How he would love growing up here, swimming in the pond in the summers, running through the leaves in the autumn, and walking the same corridors as generations of Grahams before him.

Richard's heavier footfalls brought him up beside her. "Baby May didn't want her nursemaid. She prefers me, just like her namesake."

Grace laughed. "Is that why you insisted on giving her part of my childhood nickname?"

"Of course. That, and she has your eyes. Which also explains why she loves looking at me above anyone else."

Grace rolled her eyes and lifted her free hand to stroke May's round little cheek. May giggled in response. Why, she didn't appear upset in the slightest. Grace glanced back at the carriage and caught the nursemaid playfully shaking her head. The poor woman never had a chance to do her job with Richard swooping in and ruining scheduled walks and naptimes, always eager to see his children.

There was no use complaining about it. Grace loved seeing Richard grow and thrive in his role as father. Turning back to Richard, she expected to see him hiding a laugh, but he did not meet her gaze. His childhood home stole his attention completely. She watched his eyes trail over every snow-dusted shrub to every corner of the grand manor house. He was home. He was finally home.

A cold breeze curled under her bonnet and sent a shiver down her neck. Wiping at the moisture filling her eyes, she tucked her arm through Richard's. She hated to rush him, but Oliver was right. It was freezing. "I think baby May and Oliver are eager to see their new nursery."

Oliver gave a strong tug at her arm in response.

"What? Oliver does not want to turn into an icicle?" Boyish excitement filled Richard's features as he looked expectantly at his son.

Oliver scrunched his nose. "No icicles today. I want to see my toys."

Richard groaned, winking at his son. "By all means, let the lad run ahead."

Oliver did not wait another second before bolting forward.

Their butler must've anticipated their arrival because he pushed the door open just as Oliver whipped past him. The servants lined up to welcome them, and she and Richard greeted each one of them. By the time they were all dismissed, Grace and Richard could finally take in the house again.

The large entryway was much the same besides a new rug and the vase full of fresh winter roses. But what she hadn't expected to see was the house decorated for Christmas. It was breathtaking. Richard had reluctantly handed May off to her nursemaid for a nap, and she was grateful for a moment with just him. After all this time away, there was a great deal to take in. She had practically grown up here, and memories were already flooding her mind. How much more so must it be for Richard.

Grace slipped her hand through Richard's and teased, "I hope no one is going to have a year of bad luck for hanging the evergreen boughs already."

Richard chuckled and lifted his hand to his lips. "You are married to that unlucky man."

"Hmm?" Her brow quirked. "Do you mean you arranged all of this?"

"It's a few days early, but I wanted a head start on preparing the house for our Twelfth Night party. My mother should arrive by Christmas Eve and Bridget and her husband early next week. We will be busy unpacking everything and setting the house in order, and I want them to see Belside at its finest. Not to mention . . ."

"What?"

"I wanted to surprise you."

She grinned as he pulled her to his chest. "It was a wonderful surprise. I'm so glad you are finally restored to your home."

"As am I. It feels right to have us here, especially the children." One of his hands held her securely around the waist and the other lifted to the back of her neck, his thumb gliding just under her ear. "I couldn't have done it on my own. Without Aunt Edith's inheritance, your father's guidance, my solicitor's diligence with my investments, and your resourcefulness, we wouldn't have returned so soon."

"You forget to mention your part. You worked so hard and were so disciplined with our finances. You are a credit to us, Richard."

"Thank you for being patient with me," he said. "I did it all for you and Oliver and May, and all the other children we're hopefully blessed with."

"All the other children? May is barely six months old. Don't get ahead of yourself."

Richard winked. "I like to plan ahead."

"Oh?" He had a mischievous look in his eye, and she wondered if she should be worried.

"Look up," he said.

Frowning with confusion, Grace lifted her chin, her eyes catching on a very large and very expertly arranged kissing bough hanging from the chandelier. A laugh bubbled up from her chest. "It's perfect."

"I told you on the carriage ride over that this was going to be the best Christmas our family has had yet, and that includes the decor. I insisted on the very best and the very largest kissing bough."

"Let me guess, you didn't specify any other decor, just this one."

He grinned. "You know me well. I expect a generous kiss every time we walk by it."

Grace feigned a look of ignorance. "Define generous."

"Ah, my clever minx is begging for a demonstration, and I am helpless to refuse." He dipped her back, cradling her in one arm, and *generously* kissed her.

He was right. This Christmas was shaping up to be the very best yet.

About the Author

Anneka R. Walker is a best-selling author of historical and contemporary romance. With humor and an abundance of heart, she crafts uplifting stories you won't soon forget. She is the winner of the Swoony Award, the LDSPMA Praiseworthy Award, and various chapter contests. Her books have received praise from Publishers Weekly, Historical Novel Society, Midwest Book Review, and Readers Favorite. She graduated from Brigham Young University-Idaho with a Bachelor's degree in English and history and hopes to never stop learning. She is a blessed wife, proud mother of five, follower of Jesus, connoisseur of chocolate, and believer in happy endings.

Follow the Author

I hope you enjoyed Married by Twelfth Night!
Richard and Grace were such wonderfully fun characters to write. If
you liked this book, please consider leaving a review. They are vital to
any book's success.

Stay in touch! I love connecting with my readers!

Subscribe to Anneka's Newsletter:
mailchi.mp/a278fdec4416/authorannekawalker

Facebook: @AnnekaRWalker
Instagram: @authorannekawalker

www.annekawalker.com

Also by Anneka Walker

Stand-Alone Novels:

Brides and Brothers

Love in Disguise

Refining the Debutante

Matchmaking Mamas:

Bargaining for the Barrister

An Unwitting Alliance

The Gentleman's Confession

The Rules of Matrimony

Enchanted Regency:

The Masked Baron

The Dreaming Beauty

The Lady Glass

Regency Ever After Novellas:

Her Three Suitors

Lady Mary Contrary

Christmas Books in Multi-Author series:

Merry Kismet

Married by Twelfth Night

Find A Collection Of My Novellas In Various Anthologies On Amazon.

Made in the USA
Las Vegas, NV
26 November 2024